Suzanne Loved James.

She hadn't wanted to. To think too deeply was to find the truth. She had been living an illusion but there was nothing illusory about her feelings for James. She loved him with all the facets of her nature. He had taught her passion in a way no man had; he'd given her security and caring, laughter and understanding. She had repaid him in lies.

Now, because of her, he stood in danger. She was reentering the world of shadows, of rules that had little to do with fairness. Where a life was sometimes less important than names on a list.

"Frowning this early?" James rolled over, his fingers tracing the lines between her brows. "I thought I made you happy."

She dredged up a smile. "You did." Sliding closer, she fitted her body to his. His warmth surrounded her, his scent rich and seductive. Desire spiraled within. One more time. She would taste their passion one more time.

Dear Reader:

It takes two to tango, and we've declared 1989 the "Year of the Man" at Silhouette Desire. We're honoring that perfect partner, the magnificent male, the one without whom there would be no romance. From January to December, 1989 will be a twelve-month extravaganza, spotlighting one book each month as a tribute to the Silhouette Desire hero—our *Man-of-the-Month*!

You'll find these men created by your favorite authors utterly irresistible. March, traditionally the month that "comes in like a lion and goes out like a lamb," brings a hero to match in Jennifer Greene's Mr. March, and Naomi Horton's Slater McCall is indeed a *Dangerous Kind of Man*, coming in April.

Don't let these men get away!

Yours,

Isabel Swift
Senior Editor & Editorial Coordinator

SARA CHANCE
Woman in the Shadows

Silhouette Desire
Published by Silhouette Books New York

America's Publisher of Contemporary Romance

SILHOUETTE BOOKS
300 East 42nd St., New York, N.Y. 10017

ISBN: 0-373-05485-8

First Silhouette Books printing March 1989

Printed in the U.S.A.

SARA CHANCE

lives on Florida's Gold Coast. With the ocean two minutes from home, a boat in the water in the backyard and an indoor swimming pool three feet from her word processor, is it any wonder she loves swimming, fishing and boating? Asked why she writes romance, she replies, "I live it and believe in it. After all, I met and married my husband, David, in less than six weeks." That was two teenage daughters and twenty years ago. Two of Sara's Desires, *Her Golden Eyes* and *A Touch of Passion*, were nominated by *Romantic Times* in the Best Desires category for their publishing years. And *Double Solitaire* was a Romance Writers of America Golden Medallion nominee.

One

The room was Spartan, a polished hardwood floor, bare walls, no furniture. Four men and two women moved in harmony, their slippered feet making almost no sound. The sighs of measured breathing were the only sounds heard as an ancient rite was performed. Beautiful, deadly in its ability to disarm, to kill, t'ai chi was now a form of active meditation rather than one of the first martial arts known to man. The six who moved as one knew its benefits. The small Oriental man who led the group knew its history, as well. His eyes focused on a point beyond which he could see, but he noted the position of every member of his class. A good class, no better than many with the exception of one member.

Suzanne. No last names were used here. Her red hair drew male eyes. Her body in the dark gray *gi* was slim, her legs long, strong. Her face was beautiful, quiet, unique in its ability to hide its expression. The instructor valued this woman not as a woman, but as a heart and mind to appreciate as a piece of his heritage that even many of his countrymen no longer respected. The form flowed to an end. He stood poised for a moment then bowed in the traditional way. His class bowed.

Suzanne Frazier collected her small tote from the corner by the door. They had gone through the form twice tonight. The slow easy movements looked graceful but were actually very strenuous. Her *gi*, the two-piece wrap jacket and pants, was damp with perspiration. She didn't mind, despite the fact it would be almost an hour before she would get home to shower. The small *dojo* didn't run to locker-room facilities, but she didn't mind that, either. She had been in worse places and gotten far less for her presence. Feeling at peace was as necessary now as the high caused by a rush of adrenaline had once been.

"I wish I could make my body flow with the form the way you do," Melody murmured, coming over to join Suzanne.

Suzanne smiled at the teenager. The other students were in their late twenties or thirties. "I have been working at this for three years. You've only been at it for a few months," she pointed out. She liked Melody's enthusiasm and her youthful zest. When most girls her age would have been thinking about the latest dance craze, Melody seemed intent on learning the ancient secrets of an almost forgotten knowledge.

Melody pouted, then laughed softly. "No wonder our *sensei* likes you so much. You never waste words. He's forever telling us not to waste motion and thought." She glanced at the man who taught the class. "He makes it look easy, too." Sighing, she shouldered her backpack. "One of these days he's going to watch me like he watches you. Gotta go. See you next week."

Suzanne looked at their teacher, knowing that Melody had stated no less than the truth. The *sensei* did watch her, often and with more speculation than she liked. At first she had been suspicious. Her looks had gotten her more than one unprovoked pass. But she had quickly discovered the man's interest was strictly based on her ability to perform t'ai chi. She had relaxed.

Suzanne smiled a little as she slipped down the hall toward the front entrance. She had made the break from the past. Benny had said she wouldn't be able to do it. Her smile died, on remembering her friend and mentor. Pain surfaced, disturbing the calm. She didn't fight the sensation. She accepted it then let it go so the peace would return to her again. Control. Acceptance. Ways of life that were now as much a part of her as her blue eyes.

She stopped in the doorway. The darkness outside was complete. Her senses prickled, catapulting her back in time. Adrenaline slammed into her veins. Danger! Here. On this quiet back street. Her ears strained. She heard no sound whispered to betray an alien movement. The tote bag was wrapped around her wrist. A weapon now. She flattened against the side of the door. A murmur. Her head turned. The alley. A gasp cut off. More than one. She melted back down the dimly lit hall. The exit sign at the rear of the building glowed red. She eased the door open and slid into the shadows, pausing to allow her eyes to adjust to the moonless night. She felt, more than saw, the layout of the alley.

She saw two men holding a slighter person captive between them. She closed the distance. The t'ai chi form was no longer an echo from the past, a fad practiced by the health conscious to reduce stress. Her body was a weapon.

"Hold her. I'll get the car," one of the men whispered.

A woman. Melody.

Suzanne inhaled deeply, preparing to spring the moment the man was alone with his victim. She had but a few seconds to strike. She moved forward silently, her hands slicing down to knock the man flat. Melody tumbled to the ground, screaming in terror.

Suddenly the *dojo* was alive with the sound of running feet. Suzanne slipped back the way she had come. She had no desire to advertise her part in the rescue. Let them think Melody had managed to claw her way free. She eased through the exit door. The hall was empty. Everyone was out front. She heard shouts, running, grunts of a small scuffle. The *sensei*, carrying Melody in his arms, came through the front door just as Suzanne reached it. Behind him came the other men in the class, bringing the attacker Suzanne had knocked unconscious and his accomplice. For a moment the teacher's black eyes met Suzanne's.

The sensei's gaze flickered to the back door and returned to her. Suzanne saw the knowledge of what she had done in his expression. She froze for one second, wondering if he would betray her.

"Good. I'm glad you are still here. She needs a woman."

Suzanne exhaled slowly, standing aside so that he could take Melody into the practice room. She could see the *sensei* didn't understand her reasons for hiding her part in the escape, but he intended to keep her secret. "What happened?" she asked, following the teacher to the mats rolled against one wall. She knew how to play the spectator or any of a number of other roles to perfection. She had just the right inflection to the voice, just the right expression. It was a matter of timing and training, skills developed in a past that was deliberately obscured from the present.

One of the male students answered her. "Two men tried to attack her. Somehow she got free. If you can take care of her, I'll call the police from the phone outside." The *dojo* was only a room where the martial arts students met and practiced, and it had no phone.

"It was awful," Melody sobbed, throwing herself into Suzanne's arms. Tears poured down her face as she clung to Suzanne.

Suzanne stroked her hair, trying to calm her. "It's over. You aren't hurt. It's over." She had heard enough in the alley to know how narrow Melody's escape had been. The two men had been bent on taking advantage of a young girl's vulnerability. Melody had almost become a statistic.

Melody burrowed against her. "I want my mother," she wailed. "Where is she? I need her."

"What's her number, honey? I'll call her." Suzanne would have agreed to anything at that moment to ease Melody's mind. She had been through enough.

"Oh, please hurry." Melody lifted her head and told her the number. "Don't tell Daddy. Talk to Mom."

Suzanne turned to their teacher. "Will you stay with her?"

He came down on the floor beside Melody, close but not touching. "Would it help to hold my hand?" he asked softly, extending it palm up.

Suzanne blessed him silently for his understanding of the trauma Melody was going through. "I'll be as quick as I can," she promised as soon as Melody placed her fingers hesitantly in his hand.

The street was no less dark than before. Only this time there was no danger in the shadows. Suzanne dialed the number Melody had given her. A woman answered on the third ring.

"Is she hurt?" Melody's mother demanded, breaking into Suzanne's explanation of the situation.

"Scared, probably in shock. But no physical damage that I can see."

"Thank God. I'll be there just as soon as I can," she said, fighting her tears. "Will you stay with her?"

"Of course," Suzanne replied, before realizing she was speaking to a dial tone.

James Southerland faced his brother-in-law across the width of the desk. They were fleshing out the details for his newest acquisition, a business on the verge of bankruptcy that he intended to put in the black and sell at a profit. "Let's take a break. I'm beat," he said, deciding they both could do with a drink. It was turning into a long evening, and it had already been a tiring day.

Greg smiled wearily as he massaged the tension from his neck muscles. "I'd like to, but I promised my wife, your very determined sister, that I'd get home at a decent hour for a change. It's already past nine."

Startled, James glanced at the clock. "I knew we'd been at it a while, but I didn't realize it had been this long."

"You need a wife, my friend. Believe me, you'd know what time it was every minute." Greg rose and stretched just as the phone rang.

James answered, stiffening on hearing the news his distraught sister poured into his ear. "Is she all right? She wasn't hurt?"

"No. The woman I spoke to said she was just scared. I'm leaving now for the *dojo*."

"No, wait! Greg and I will stop by and pick you up."

"Forget it. Why do you think I didn't ask to speak to Greg? He'd have said the same thing. Melody needs me. I'm on my way out the door. Now!"

James slammed up the receiver, realizing Laurie was gone. "Damn!"

Greg stared at him. "What's wrong?"

"Two men tried to grab Melody after t'ai chi class. She's all right, but Laurie is going over there now. She won't wait for us to pick her up." As he spoke, he was pulling on his jacket and heading for the door. Greg was right on his heels.

"Damn, Laurie is as stubborn as they come. I didn't want Melody to take lessons from that place. I never did like that area of town. I never should have let those two gang up on me and convince me Melody would be all right," Greg lamented.

Both men got into James's car. "Don't be a fool. It's no more your fault than it is theirs. Melody pleaded with you for months to take t'ai chi. And the teacher does have a very good reputation. We checked, remember? No one could have foreseen this."

Greg slumped against the seat. "I know. But Melody? What she must be feeling. And Laurie."

The car sped through the night as both men lapsed into silence. The drive seemed longer than it was. James parked the car in front of the *dojo*. The street was crawling with police cars and spectators. Glaring at the carnival-type atmosphere, he stalked through the maze to the front entrance of the small building. An officer stopped him.

"You can't go in there, sir."

"I can. That's my daughter in there," Greg announced belligerently, having reached the entrance first.

James caught his arm when he looked ready to push his way in. "I'm Melody's uncle," he added in a quieter tone. He was no less angry than Greg, but he had spent too many years controlling his temper to allow it to win now.

The officer stepped back with an apology. The scene inside the *dojo* was much quieter. Four men and a detective stood off to one side. Laurie was on the floor across the room, holding a sobbing Melody in her arms. Beside her knelt a red-haired woman. The teacher was answering questions put to him by a stocky policeman. James noticed the details even as he closed the distance to his sister and niece. Greg moved faster, going onto his knees beside his family. He nearly knocked the red-haired woman over in his haste. James reached out intending to steady her, but she was quicker. In a catlike move she was on her feet and a half step away. Distracted, James watched her for a moment. Her attention was on Melody. She hardly noticed him, or so he thought until his gaze settled on her face. Light blue eyes stared straight at him, cataloging everything about him. The feeling was new, for the look had none of the sexual interest that he was accustomed to getting from the women he met. This was an assessment in its simplest form. Irritated that this unknown female could capture his interest in the midst of a crisis, he turned his attention to his niece. It was a while before Melody had spilled out her tale and been soothed by her parents. Only then did James allow himself to look around the room and discover the woman was gone. He frowned, not liking the disappointment he felt. I must be more tired than I thought, he decided as he followed Greg and his family from the building. He never had been interested in red-haired women. Usually they were too temperamental for his tastes. He liked class, poise, calm in the midst of a storm—not emotional highs and lows.

* * *

Suzanne guided her car into the small garage at the rear of her house. The sound of another car pulling in behind hers startled her for a second. She smiled, recognizing her friend Pat's bright yellow Volkswagen.

"I thought you weren't coming back to town until tomorrow," Suzanne said, getting out.

Pat laughed. "I wasn't, until that crazy photographer tried to convince me an affair was just what the doctor ordered to mend my broken heart."

Despite the sleek though diminutive look of a professional model, Pat acted the part of an exuberant puppy. She didn't glide, she bounced. With her background and well-traveled history, she should have been bored or even a little jaded. Instead she was plainly enthusiastic about anything and everything, finding joy with the unself-consciousness of a child. She was Suzanne's direct opposite, and Suzanne liked Pat for all her contrasts. Her own cynicism needed the leavening of Pat's trust. Her reserve and caution found an outlet in just watching Pat barrel through life at top speed.

"So what did you tell your amorous male?"

Pat tried to match Suzanne's long stride, knowing as she did it was a wasted effort. "You should be the model, not me. Slow down, will you! Five-foot-three women don't have the long legs of five-foot-ten-inch females. Give me a break." She nearly ran over Suzanne when she shortened her stride.

"That's the second time tonight someone's tried to mow me down," Suzanne murmured absently.

"Oh. How?" Pat shifted her luggage to her other hand while she waited for Suzanne to open the door of the house they shared.

"I'll answer you as soon as you answer me."

"Rats. I was hoping you wouldn't notice my adroit sidestepping." Pat made a face. "I should have known better. You never miss anything. Offer me a cup of coffee at your place, and I'll give you all the gory details."

Suzanne glanced at her, for the first time seeing the strain in her expression. "Did you forget to stock the cupboard again before you left?"

"Don't I always. I'm not the world's most organized person." She headed down the hall. "Give me ten minutes."

Suzanne stared after her, frowning. Pat had been so excited when Mitch had noticed her, singling her out to model for a layout he was doing for a major cosmetics company. After one relationship gone sour, Pat had been working at being cautious. Mitch had been determined. Finally Pat had accepted a date. Soon they were more than friends but not quite lovers. Then the shooting assignment had been changed from New Orleans to Houston.

Suzanne went up the stairs to her own apartment, wondering what could have happened. She had met and liked Mitch. He was quiet, gentle and, above all, seemed genuinely fond of Pat. She put the coffee on to perk then decided to take a shower. When she finished, she found Pat waiting in the living room, the pot and cups on the low table in front of the couch.

"I made myself at home."

"So I see." Suzanne tossed three of the giant cushions that lay tumbled on the window seat to the floor. When given a choice, she rarely sat on the sofa. She took the cup Pat handed her, waiting for Pat to begin.

"I blew it. I actually believed he cared about me," Pat blurted.

Suzanne's brows rose, but she said nothing.

"I went to Houston, knowing that before I got back we'd be lovers. I wanted him. He wanted me. It was crazy especially after Todd, but I thought, okay, a woman can think she's in love, then find out she was wrong and really fall in love in less than six months. It is possible." She drank the last of her coffee down in one swallow. "We went to bed all right, and then the next morning he told me about his wife and two little girls."

Suzanne's hands clenched tight on her cup. She swore silently and hung on to her temper with effort. Pat needed an ear, not an angry friend. "I take it you told him what you thought of him."

"You got it in one. For once in my life, I didn't have a bit of trouble thinking of words nasty enough for the situation. Then I packed my bags and hightailed it for here. Thank heavens the shoot was over. My big break professionally, and it had to come from this louse. At my age, a moderately successful model can't afford to be too choosy. The rotten part about the whole deal is, if the company likes the layout, I'll be doing a promo tour and Mitch will be going along. How the devil am I going to get through that? I'll be darned if I'm going to let him mess this up for me. I want this assignment badly. It'll give me enough money to buy one of these old houses and turn it into apartments like you've done. I'll have a roof over my head and a steady income all in one shot. Then I'll be able to sink the rest of my savings into that little boutique I want." She set her cup down with a clatter and jumped to her feet to pace to the window and back. "I feel like a fool."

Suzanne watched her, hurting for her. Pat's ability to trust people left her open for so much pain. For one moment she remembered another woman a long time ago. She, too, believed in trusting and taking chances. And she had been hurt. Not heartbroken, but worse—angry, disillusioned, lost. The pain started to build. Suzanne forced it down and concentrated on the present. The past was gone, it could only touch her if she allowed it. "You shouldn't. He's the fool, not you."

"I got taken in by a pretty face."

"I wouldn't exactly call Mitch a pretty face."

Despite herself, Pat smiled a little. "All right, so I exaggerated a bit. You don't know what it's like. I don't think you've ever made a mistake in your life. You sit there all sleek and elegant, making the rest of us look like cows, and you smile that smile of yours. Nothing ever seems to get to you. You don't ever get angry, excited, depressed or irritable."

Suzanne stood and stretched. "You think so? You don't know me very well." Sometimes, in the dark of the night, she remembered feeling all those things and more.

"Correction. You mean you don't allow me to know you very well. In fact I don't think you allow anyone to know you. Look at this apartment. All the rooms that anyone would see are beautifully light, spacious places. Original art on the walls, Waterford crystal, dhurrie rugs, antiques and art everywhere.''

"I *am* in the import-export business," Suzanne pointed out dryly, glancing around at the decor.

Pat waved the comment away. "Then there is your bedroom. You don't look the type to fall in love with a house that spent most of its youth as a high-class brothel. And you certainly don't look the type to have the first floor and half of the second remodeled with the latest conveniences, while keeping most of the furnishings and the aura of the house intact in your bedroom. Blue velvet and silver tassels. I almost choked when I saw it the first time."

"I'll grant you, it's gaudy—"

"And campy and very risqué."

"But where's your sense of humor?"

"I left it in Houston." Pat threw herself on the couch, her face contorting with disillusionment.

Suzanne sat down beside her and put her arms around her shoulders. "Forget him, Pat. You tried your best to be sure, and it just wasn't in the cards for you. Mitch was a mistake, but you walked away. He cost you. I know he did. Still it's over now but for the crying."

"It would have been bad enough if it had only been a wife. But two children. I hate myself."

Suzanne's hands tightened, and she shook Pat once, hard enough to get her attention. "Stop that. It's not your fault. Guilt accomplishes nothing."

Pat's tears started then. She buried her face in her hands and cried. Suzanne eased her friend back on the cushions and let her grieve, knowing the process would heal her far faster than any words. And when it was over, she offered Pat the couch and a blanket for the night.

The clash of metal against metal penetrated Suzanne's sleep. She awoke abruptly, instantly alert. The sound came again, followed by a muted oath. Pat, she realized, was in the kitchen. She relaxed and yawned. Stretching, she lay back in bed for a moment. Another day in the life of Suzanne Frazier. More banging of pottery, another oath, at least three words she didn't recognize, then silence. The absence of sound disturbed her more than the noise. Pat was no good at cooking. Getting up, she grabbed a robe and headed for the kitchen. *Disaster in the making* should have been the title of the scene that greeted her.

"What are you doing?" she asked, leaning against the doorjamb.

"I thought I would cook breakfast as a kind of thank-you for listening to my tale of woe last night." Pat glanced at the mess she had made. "I think it would have been kinder to plant a bomb in here. I know it would have been neater." One blackened skillet, still smoking, sat on a burner too large for it. The blender, minus its lid, held a pinkish concoction both in it and splattered on the wall behind it. The toaster, fortunately unplugged, had a knife sticking out of it.

"The table looks nice."

Pat grimaced. "My one and only claim to fame in the culinary world. I can set a table like a pro."

"You wash and I'll cook. You may be my favorite friend, but I positively won't clean up after you." Suzanne pushed away from the door and went to the stove. "Mushroom omelet, okay?"

"I'll eat anything. I'm starving."

Suzanne glanced at her sharply. "I take it you're feeling better."

"You were right. I'm bent up a little, but I'll survive. Thanks for holding my hand. Being alone last night would have been the straw on the camel's back."

"Forget it. You'd do the same for me."

Pat laughed slightly. "Not unless you've got a man stashed around I don't know about." She filled the sink with soap and water. "Which reminds me. You never did tell me how you got run over last night. And when."

"We had a bit of excitement at t'ai chi. One of the group was accosted in the alley after class. The girl, Melody."

"The one who thinks you're superlady."

Startled, Suzanne looked at her. "I never told you that."

"I may be stupid where men are concerned, but I can read between the lines with you sometimes. So who ran you down? One of the bad guys?"

"Not likely. The guys at the *dojo* had them well in hand. Actually it was Melody's father." She stared off into space, remembering the man with him. He hadn't been any less angry than the father, but he had been far more controlled. Of the two men, she would have wagered the second was more dangerous when crossed than the first. Annoyed with herself for thinking in those terms, she concentrated on the eggs in the skillet.

"Surely the father isn't putting that look on your face. I thought you told me Melody lives with both her parents, her married parents."

"She does. And I don't have any special look."

"Oh, no? Pull the other one. Unless there was someone else there?" Pat eyed her speculatively.

The man had been intriguing, she had to admit. His image was certainly lingering in her mind with more clarity than she liked. "There were a lot of someones."

"Who was he? One of the class?"

His eyes had been dark, shrewd and his body muscled, with the look of a man who knew fitness was more than lifting weights in a fancy gym. She had definitely noticed too much. Old habits, she consoled herself, trying to believe that was all her interest was. "You're like a bulldog when you get an idea in your head."

"Give."

"All right. There was a man with the father. I think I heard someone say his name was Southerland. I didn't catch the first name." He had been taller than she, lean without being rangy.

"Too bad it wasn't James Southerland. That's one sexy man. He's single, wealthy, successful, ambitious and smart. He's got the most gorgeous brown hair and eyes I've ever seen."

Brown was a bland description for his eyes. They were more the shade of rich imported chocolate. "I think we're talking about the same man. When did you meet him?''

"At a party. He was with a dynamite-looking blonde who acted like she had won the lottery. The guy's a great dancer, too. Made the rest of the men there look like robots. Had every woman in the place green with envy. Wouldn't it be great if he called you and asked you out.''

Suzanne flipped the second of the omelets. "Not very likely. If it was James Southerland, he doesn't even know my name.''

"That kind of man would have no trouble finding it out.''

"You're a dreamer. That kind of thing is standard fare in the movies.''

Pat laughed, the first natural bit of humor she had displayed. "And you're a cynic. Blue-eyed redheads with eye-popping figures make most men forget their manners and remember their cavemen skills.''

Suzanne placed the two plates with the omelets on the table. "Sit down, be quiet and eat,'' she commanded, refusing to take Pat seriously. She lived a subdued life by choice. A man like Southerland most likely didn't. She wouldn't think any further than that. Excitement, the thrill of the chase was an addiction she had beaten. No man, no job, no situation was going to resurrect the need. "I have to go to work even if you don't. The European order comes in today.''

Two

Suzanne negotiated the traffic of downtown New Orleans. Her shop, Unique, Inc., was located on a narrow side street. Its lacy grillwork, small courtyard with flowers and two-story look was a visual piece of New Orleans's history. In contrast, the inside of the shop was definitely modern. Walls had been knocked down to make big rooms out of small ones. Europe, the East, the Orient, South America and slices of North American creativity came together in a brotherhood of art. Paintings, pottery, sculpture, crafts—some, products of old almost-forgotten skills, some, experiments with high-tech ingenuity. All were available under one roof for a price. Suzanne traveled the world she knew so well, searching for the different, the special, the unique. Her clients were as varied as her merchandise. Her reputation was solid. Her expertise and eye for the original was intuitive and skilled. She had made herself and her world to her own tastes. Few knew how very single-minded she could be. None suspected her reasons for the life she led and the way she could move in and out of countries so easily.

"Good morning, Suzanne."

She smiled at Darin, her assistant. Attractive in a quiet way, in his mid-twenties, slim and tanned, he was an asset to the shop with his charm and the contacts he brought from the wealthy society of the city of which he was a part. "You're in early." Actually he was always there before her. He had visions of a partnership someday, and he wasn't above working to achieve his dream. Suzanne respected his drive, knowing he would make a good future partner.

"I wanted to be here in case the truck was early."

She laughed. "Tell the truth. You were hoping it would get here ahead of schedule so you could start without me."

He gave her a sharp look. "Do you really believe that? I know I haven't been exactly subtle about wanting to buy into this place—"

"No, you haven't," she agreed. "But if I didn't trust you, you wouldn't have gotten in the door, and I certainly wouldn't have made you my assistant." She entered her office with him on her heels. "Unique has quite a reputation. It wouldn't be difficult to replace you if that's what I wanted to do." Sitting down, she leaned back in her chair, watching him. She had been a bit leery of hiring him at first. His moneyed background could have made him think the world owed him a free ride. He had proved her wrong, working as hard as she and with just as much determination.

"You know I don't think I'll ever get used to your bluntness. You look like a loud word would offend you, and yet you don't soft sell anything. I've seen you deal with overbearing customers, soothing them like fractious children, and yet you can beat down a hustler in a second." He took the chair across from her. "You are one deceptive-looking woman."

He was shrewd, too. One of these days he just might figure her out. For an instant she welcomed the challenge of foxing him, then just as quickly she put the temptation away. "And you've got a glib tongue."

"I'm learning." He grinned, hazel eyes glinting behind the frame of his glasses. "I'm glad you know what I want. I've been trying for months to tell you and couldn't think of a way without sounding like a fool. What could I possibly bring to this place that you don't already have?"

"Money, for one thing," she murmured dryly.

Darin waved that away as if it weren't important. "My family's, not mine. I could get the bucks to buy in, we both know that. But it's the knowledge, the expertise I really want. You're good. I want to be that good."

"What makes you think you aren't?"

He laughed, shaking his head. "For one thing, the fact that I almost got taken in by that reproduction last week."

"It was a very good repro."

"Not good enough to fool you."

"Experience."

"Intuition and some kind of feel for it, as well. I watched your face. You knew almost from the moment you picked it up."

Suzanne glanced down, neither denying nor agreeing with his assessment. The statue had been beautiful. Its lack of antiquity hadn't detracted from that. Even now it sat on a shelf at home, but not for the price its greedy owner had demanded. She smiled a little, remembering the man's shock at being found out.

"Do you think I have a chance of developing that kind of instinct?"

"Yes." She looked up, seeing the hope in his eyes. He wanted his dream so badly he was willing to slave for it. She remembered the feeling, sympathized with it, even as she knew she was glad her dreaming days were over.

"Two years, maybe less. Junior status. I can't promise you more."

"You mean it?" He leaned forward in his seat, a man straining at the leash of his own limitations.

"Have you ever known me to say something I don't mean?"

"No way." He jumped to his feet. "Damn, I wish I had some champagne. I feel like celebrating."

"Save it. We still have the European order due in."

Darin came around the desk and yanked her out of the chair. Before Suzanne could react, he had her in his arms, swinging her around. "You just wait. I'm going to be the best junior partner you ever had." He dipped his head, kissing her on the mouth. He dropped his arms, a shocked look on his face. "Tell me I didn't just do that."

Only Suzanne's quick reflexes saved her from an awkward landing. "Put it down to excessive enthusiasm," she suggested, smiling a little to ease his embarrassment.

"You're a brick. Thank God, you aren't one of those excitable females, or I'd be in the suds." He backed out of the room. "I've got some work to do in the storeroom. Can you watch the front?"

"He didn't even wait for an answer," Suzanne murmured, shaking her head. "A brick, am I." She had been called a lot of things in her life, but that was a first. Just for a moment she wondered what Darin or Pat would have thought of her had they been able to see her in her old life. Calm, controlled Suzanne had existed, but she certainly hadn't been as visible. The Suzanne of the past had lived on the edge. She had worked in the shadows, had known the night more intimately than the day and had slept lightly, aware that friends were not always what they seemed.

"I would have shocked them both."

"There's a call for you on line two," Darin announced, poking his head around the storeroom door.

Suzanne looked up from the crate she was unpacking, grimacing at the interruption. "Important?"

"Not sure. Said it was about somebody named Melody. I explained you were busy. The woman said she'd call back, but she sounded funny so I took a chance. Was I wrong?"

"No. I'll take it in my office." Worried at the un-precedented call, Suzanne picked up the phone while taking a seat. She just had time to identify herself before the woman on the line spoke.

"Ms. Frazier, I'm Laurie Gibson, Melody's mother. I didn't mean to bother you at work, but I wanted to thank you for what you did for Melody last night. And for calling me. She has told us so much about you since she started taking t'ai chi that I feel I know you a little." She paused to take a breath, strangely nervous. "I don't usually run on like this," she apologized.

"First of all, I didn't really do anything. Just provided a bit a moral support until you could arrive. No thanks are necessary," Suzanne said quietly, feeling uncomfortable because Laurie was. She hadn't expected to hear from Melody's parents. "How is Melody?" she asked, hoping to ease the situation.

"Better today. We kept her home from school, of course. Thank goodness, tomorrow is Saturday. Which is really why I'm calling. I wondered, if you aren't busy tonight, if you would come by for dinner. I would really like a chance to meet you. Greg, that's my husband, feels the same."

"That's not nece—"

"Are you busy?" Laurie asked, interrupting.

"No, but—"

"Please say you'll come. I know I'm not handling this at all well. I don't usually sound as if I don't have a brain." She sighed audibly. "The truth is, I would like to know you. You've impressed Melody. Even before this happened, I wanted to meet you, but I just couldn't figure out how to go about it," she confessed.

Suzanne hesitated. A night out would be nice, and she did like Melody, and she did want to be sure the teenager was really recovering. "All right. I'd like to come."

"Seven?" Laurie offered before Suzanne could change her mind.

"Fine."

She hung up, wondering at Laurie's insistence and her own rationalized agreement. On the face of it, the invitation wasn't that unusual given the circumstances.

"Problems, Suzanne?"

She glanced up. "No. Just someone who thinks they owe me something."

"But I need you to make up the numbers," Laurie argued. "I swear, James, you are the most provoking brother alive. We owe this woman our thanks. It isn't too much to have her to dinner. I would think you would want to express your appreciation, too. Melody is your one and only niece."

James frowned at the phone, wishing Laurie could see him. "I'm buried under a pile of contracts. You know I'm in the middle of a messy business deal. You've been grumping enough about Greg's overtime. I need to work tonight."

"Take a break. You know you need one. You can work tomorrow if you must. Come to dinner. Please."

"Wheedling won't work now like it did when you were little. I remember Mom saying how you always got your way with that trick. I'm not buying it."

"I need you."

Suspicious, for his older sister rarely said that to anyone but Greg, he demanded, "Why?"

Laurie sighed. "Greg has put his foot down. He says, no more t'ai chi. You know how Melody feels about that. You know how hard she fought to get a chance to take lessons from that teacher. She's kept up her schoolwork. She's done everything Greg asked, and now this. It wasn't her fault. God knows I'm worried about that neighborhood at night. But she wants it so, and the man is a good teacher. I need you to help me. I was hoping this Suzanne would, as well."

"You don't even know the woman," he argued.

"No, but Melody does. She thinks Suzanne might be willing to let her ride with her to class. Melody says she lives fairly close to us."

"It sounds to me like Melody says far too much. This woman has her own life. She doesn't want to be saddled with a teenager, no matter how engaging."

"We don't know that."

James sighed, raking his fingers through his hair. "Did I ever tell you that you're stubborn? What's wrong with you taking Melody and picking her up?"

"She's a senior. You don't know how girls are at that age. They don't want Mommy and Daddy hanging around their necks. Say you'll come."

"All right. But don't expect me to do anything but sit there. This whole thing sounds odd."

"She's coming at seven."

"I'll be there."

James hung up, debating the merits of pretending he was an orphan. Laurie and her lone chick were enough to give a sane man gray hair. How conservative, never-put-a-foot-wrong Greg ever fell in love with his complex, never-do-anything-the-easy-way sister was beyond him. If he ever got married, it would be to a woman who made his life easier, less hectic. She could have her own career. He was smart enough to realize the modern woman needed more to stimulate her than babies and hubby home at five for dinner. But he needed a haven to come home to. His schedule was packed to overflowing most days. Having a thrill-seeking, chaos-oriented mate would be his idea of misery. No, give him a logical, orderly woman, intelligent, attractive—she didn't have to be beautiful—reasonably interested in her home and maybe a child or two, and he would be happy.

Suzanne dressed for the evening, choosing one of her favorite outfits. Soft cream silk draped across her shoulders leaving her arms bare. The neckline dipped in delicate gathers front and back. A nipped-in waist above a shirred skirt finished a swishy, feminine look. She left her hair loose, a cloud of red curls to brush her shoulders. Preferring understatement in her jewelry, jade earrings were her only ornamentation.

The drive to the Gibson house was short, her present and past professional successes having provided her with a better-than-average address. Laurie answered the door, the man Suzanne recognized as Melody's father a step behind her.

"What a lovely dress," Laurie said, smiling as she took the matching jacket. "This is my husband, Greg." She looked beyond Suzanne to the man just coming through the door. "And this is my brother, James Southerland. We never did get to introductions last night."

Suzanne turned slowly, finding herself the target of those eyes again. This time there was admiration in the dark depths, curiosity and interest. She held out her hand. His fingers enfolded hers, bringing warmth and a sense of strength to the conventional gesture.

"Ms. Frazier." James found himself reacting when he hadn't expected to. Seeing her the night before hadn't prepared him for the elegance, the poise that radiated from her now. She met his eyes, neither looking away nor flirting. She stood tall, coming almost to his chin. He liked that. The regal carriage, the soft voice, the firm touch of her hand against his. Intriguing. Definitely intriguing. The irritation at being taken from his work gave way to pleasure.

"Suzanne." Melody came down the stairs in a rush. "Sorry I'm late, but I overslept. Mom insisted I take a nap today." She grimaced affectionately as she joined her parents.

Suzanne took the opportunity of Melody's arrival to withdraw her hand from James's grasp. She had come to share a meal and had found excitement in a man's touch. Curls of anticipation wrapped around her. James was clearly interested, and oddly she was reacting far more strongly than she had in a long time. Caging her wayward senses, she turned to Melody.

"How are you?"

"Fine, but no one believes me. I can't wait for class next week. Remember the *sensei* told us how t'ai chi used to be a form of defense. Well, I must have learned more than I thought, or I wouldn't have been able to get away." She frowned. "Although I sure don't remember what I did."

"That's enough talk about t'ai chi," Greg said, speaking for the first time. "We agreed you'd take some time off from it."

"You agreed. I didn't." Melody glanced at her father, her happy mood turning rebellious. "I know you don't want me to go to that class, but even you have to admit what I'm learning came in handy."

Greg's eyes glittered at her tone. "We won't discuss this now. Our guests are standing in the hall." He gestured toward the doors to his left, clearly making an effort at hospitality.

"Yes, come in, please," Laurie rushed to add. "I don't know what you'll be thinking of us, Suzanne. I may call you Suzanne?"

"Of course," she said, feeling sorry for Melody and her parents. It was clear t'ai chi was a bone of contention in the household.

"My niece isn't usually so rag mannered." James touched Melody's shoulder, consoling and correcting her at the same time.

Melody smiled at him. "I get too enthusiastic sometimes," she admitted.

"What will you have to drink?" Greg stood at the small bar.

"White wine would be fine."

"I'll take a Scotch." James took a seat beside Suzanne on the couch. The small talk had given him time to maneuver her into using the sofa instead of one of many chairs in the room. He watched her respond to his family, listening to the easy way she smoothed over Melody's little battle and drew his sister out. She charmed without seeming to. Even Greg was looking less annoyed. The transition from the living room to the dining room was smooth. The food was excellent, as always. He ate without paying much attention to what he put into his mouth.

Her manners were flawless. She listened to everyone, contributed enough to draw each out and still said little about herself. His curiosity deepened. She was quiet but not self-effacing. There was strength in her, yet he doubted anyone at the table but him realized it. She dealt with Melody's clear case of hero worship tactfully.

For her part, Suzanne was aware of James, too aware of him for her peace of mind. Every move she made was under scrutiny. The more he watched her the more careful she became.

"Suzanne, I want to ask you for a favor. My mother will tell you I haven't any manners, but this is important to me," Melody said.

"No, you don't, young lady," Greg muttered, giving his only child a glare that should have stopped her.

"Melody, you promised," Laurie murmured, looking distracted.

Suzanne glanced at James, waiting for his objection to join the rest. For once he wasn't looking at her. His eyes were on his niece as he spoke. "I know what you're going to say. I have a solution. I'll take you to and from class if it means that much to you."

Suzanne turned to Melody. The light shining in the girl's eyes told the whole story. "You mean it. You won't led Dad talk you out of it?" Melody said enthusiastically.

Even with her limited knowledge of James Southerland, Suzanne could have told her that no one talked him out of anything unless he wanted it that way. She held her peace, preferring to listen.

"I mean it. Your father is only worried about the neighborhood. It never has been the classes themselves."

"But our *sensei* is the best," Melody wailed.

"We know that, honey." Greg added his part, looking very relieved. "It was the only reason I agreed to this in the first place. But the man is an eccentric. Just because he started on a shoestring in that neighborhood is no reason he couldn't have moved when he built up his business."

"We're not always like this," Laurie apologized.

Suzanne smiled slightly. "I didn't think you were. I take it Melody wanted me to take her to class with me?" Suzanne commented in a low tone that escaped notice in the discussion going on between the men and Melody.

Laurie shifted in embarrassment. This woman was quicker than she looked. "It was my idea, I'm afraid. And it was very presumptuous. But Greg..." She gestured helplessly. "And he's right, especially after last night. She wants it so."

"She's very good."

Laurie's eyes lit up. "Is she?"

Suzanne nodded. "I don't know much about raising children, but I would think the discipline would be good for her, as well."

"I heard that," Melody teased, pleased at having saved her classes. "I wish we were dressed for a little practice. Mom, you should see Suzanne. She's really good."

James studied her, easily picturing her moving through the controlled positions. T'ai chi had been nothing more than a word to him until Greg had started investigating what he had thought was his daughter's latest craze. "I'd like to see you perform sometime," he said, driven by an impulse to rattle her.

Suzanne let her eyes slide over him before settling on his face. She knew a challenge when she heard it. "I don't perform in public," she returned. She waited a beat and continued; timing was everything. "My form of t'ai chi is strictly a solitary pursuit."

"I understood there are dual forms, as well."

"I've never learned those." She smiled as she delivered the final coup.

James smiled, too. She had not disappointed him. So often women were predictable. This one had everything he had ever wanted in a partner and an added bonus of a quickness of mind that matched his own. Pleased with their first encounter, he set his mind to arranging a second. The conventional invitation to dinner wouldn't do. The lady was cool. She would need a touch of finesse. Melody was his opening. For whatever reason, she had taken a liking to his niece.

For Suzanne the evening could have ended there, although it lasted for an hour longer. Melody wandered off to call one of her friends. The surprisingly lively conversation between the four adults made the time pass quickly. Suzanne decided she had enjoyed herself. She drove home wondering if James could say the same. It had been a long time since a man had challenged her in more than a superficial way. She wasn't averse to a little light flirtation, but she didn't think that was what James had in mind. His looks were entirely too intense, too dissecting. And his remarks about t'ai chi. Double entendre, both. What would his next move be? She had half expected a dinner invitation, been braced to refuse. It hadn't come even when he had walked her out to her car. He had been courteous but not in the least personal. He had opened and closed her car door, neither lingering nearby to prolong the simple gesture nor hurrying away.

The man had superb timing. He moved smoothly through conversations and courtesies almost as gracefully as he stalked through life. In another time and another place, she would have met him without a qualm. She would have played the game he obviously knew so well. Today she knew better. He represented danger of a different kind. So she would retreat. The hunter can't hunt when there is no quarry, she assured herself before falling asleep.

Three

———

"May I help you?" Darin paused a few feet from the tall man inspecting the display of Peruvian pottery.

James turned at the question. "I was looking for Suzanne Frazier."

"She's not here at the moment. I'm her assistant, Darin Littlefield. Is there something I can show you?"

James stifled a feeling of irritation. His impulse wasn't turning out the way it should have. "I had hoped to talk to her." When Darin continued to wait for more of an explanation, James added, "We met at dinner at my sister's last night." He couldn't remember the last time he had faced someone protecting a woman he was interested in.

Darin studied him and nodded. "She's at an auction."

"Where?"

"Beaulieu's"

"How long?"

"Since ten this morning."

"Then she should be ready for lunch."

Darin shook his head, smiling a little. "Don't count on it."

James grinned, his eyes lighting with determination. "Want to bet?"

Darin looked him over and matched his grin. "You don't know her very well."

"I want to." The man might be younger than he was, but it was best to have the lines clear.

"If that's a warning, don't bother. I'm no competition, Mr. Southerland."

James's brows rose.

"You're very photogenic, or at least the newspaper photographers think so," Darin pointed out. "Besides, my father would like to see me emulate your example."

James glanced around the shop. "You own a piece of this?"

Darin laughed. "Not yet. I'm working on it." He too looked around the store. "She doesn't need a partner, but she's willing to take me on in a few years," he said more to himself than to James.

James's curiosity deepened a few more notches. He had recognized Darin's name and jumped to the obvious and erroneous conclusion that the Littlefields were silent partners in Unique, Inc. An operation the size of Suzanne's didn't come cheaply. Deciding that any questions he had would be better put to the lady herself, James took his leave.

Beaulieu's Auction House was across town in one of the older sections of New Orleans. From the outside, the building resembled an old Southern mansion. The inside held antique treasures that drew dealers and collectors. The atmosphere was subdued yet vibrantly alive as the select crowd seated before a small stage bid for the various pieces offered. It only took a few seconds for James to spot the distinctive crown of red hair. The artificial light shot the tumbled mass with gold. It was a wonder to him that any man in the place could keep his mind on business. His eyes narrowed as he saw her hand move in a discreet gesture. She was bidding. He glanced at the platform. The carved jade horse being held by the auctioneer was stunning. Exquisitely wrought, the satiny green stone reflected shards of light so that the horse seemed to live in the frozen pose of a half rear.

James flicked his fingers, entering the bidding on an impulse. Beaulieu's clientele was by invitation only, unless one knew the owners as he did. He looked to Suzanne, but since he stood three rows behind her, she hadn't seen him. Her hand moved again. James raised the ante. Suzanne raised it again. James almost let her have the horse but changed his mind just before the auctioneer brought the gavel down on the sale. He raised, and when he upped the price again, Suzanne turned in her seat. He caught her surprise in the flash of her eyes before she faced forward once more. He smiled to himself. He didn't need to see her face to know she was hooked. The set of her head and the sudden stiffening of her spine were more eloquent than words.

Suzanne smoldered as she raised the price again. She had reached her limit for this piece. She wanted the horse badly, and if anyone but James had been bidding on it, she would have let it go. She didn't want to feel this surge of competitiveness, but she couldn't deny its existence. This stranger had a lot to answer for. She wasn't given to impulses anymore, yet she upped the price again.

James raised as he walked slowly down the aisle toward Suzanne's seat. He ignored the murmurs of interest his bidding and presence created. His attention didn't waver from the woman who now could have looked at him by turning her head slightly. She never missed a beat. She drew the waiting out to the last second then inserted her bid. He matched her, waiting for her to give up. She didn't. The game stopped being fun. He glanced at the horse, realizing he had pushed the price so high the whole room was buzzing. He looked back at her face. Nothing showed on its smooth surface. Suzanne could have been sitting in an empty room for all the emotion she showed. James frowned. It was his turn. The auctioneer was waiting. The audience was on the edge of its collective seat. He could afford the exorbitant price, but could she? The thought of losing, something that rarely happened in his life, was little compared to what he might have done with his little game. He had not meant to humble her or take something she valued. He had meant to intrigue, to pique her curiosity.

"Going!" One strike.

A moment of silence. Suzanne held her breath. Perhaps he was copying her actions.

"Going!" Two strikes of the gavel.

James started to raise his hand and at the last moment changed his mind. He shook his head instead.

"Gone!"

Suzanne expelled her breath, her hands flexing out of their carefully relaxed pose. She had won. She turned her head and found him watching her. Was that an apology she saw in his eyes? The woman beside her rose and left. James came forward and took the empty seat. Their eyes met and held.

"I don't like to lose. Pride is a damnable thing in a man when he forgets how to back down," he murmured.

Suzanne had fielded many passes in her life. Looking the way she did, she had always captured more than an average share of male interest. But she had never met a man like James. With those few words he slipped beneath her defenses.

"Men aren't the only ones with pride," she returned just as quietly.

"Let me make up the difference in the price you meant to pay and what I pushed you into," he offered, daring offending her in an effort to redress his behavior.

She smiled, shaking her head. "No," she refused, politely, firmly. "It was my choice to fight it out with you. The price of my pride."

Integrity. Another quality he valued. "Then let me take you to lunch." Although the auctioneer was taking a short break, they spoke in near whispers.

She shook her head, refusing again.

"Why? Is there a man who would object?"

"I don't have to give you a reason."

"Is it me?"

"You should know better. You dress yourself and shave every day. What is there about you I could object to?"

He waved his physical appearance away as though it didn't exist. Her bluntness surprised him, but he didn't have time to think about it. He wanted her agreement now more than ever. "You know that's not what I meant." The irritation lacing his voice came as a surprise.

"I am aware of your reputation."

He studied her, not certain which reputation she referred to. "Personally? Business? I wasn't aware either was unacceptable."

Suzanne sat back in her chair, wondering why she was prolonging their conversation. She had intended to put him off, not increase his interest. "I'll be honest. I don't want to be involved with you. It has nothing really to do with you. It's me and what I want. You don't fit."

James's eyes narrowed.

She read the building anger and sighed. "I lead a quiet life by choice. Yours is anything but. Every woman you're with becomes news. I like my privacy."

He considered her words carefully, finding truth in them. "And if I promise you privacy?"

Suzanne blinked. The determination in his voice was crystal clear. The look in his eyes reinforced his seriousness. Curious, she forgot for a moment she didn't want the risk he represented. "Are you always this single-minded about a woman who takes your fancy?''''

"No."

She waited for an explanation. When it didn't come, she probed, "Why me?"

He smiled, knowing he had finally accomplished what he had set out to do. He had gotten her to move toward him instead of away. "Come to lunch with me and find out."

She intended to say no. "All right. I've spent my limit anyway." She rose, wondering if she had taken leave of her senses. Challenges. Would she ever learn to ignore them?

James's hand cupped her elbow as they moved down the aisle to the small desk where Suzanne would pay for the horse. He stood beside her while she wrote the check. Even the beauty of the jade sculpture didn't relieve his feelings of guilt over his part in the sale.

"I wish you would let me pay the difference," he muttered as they stepped into the sunlight.

Suzanne stopped, turning toward him with a frown on her face. "If you are going to spend our lunch worrying over this, don't. Believe me, I'll get my money back when it's sold. The profit won't be as great, perhaps, but I won't lose anything."

He had his answer. She was right, she wouldn't lose. He would see to that if he had to buy the jade from her himself.

"All right, pretty lady. I'll quit bringing the subject up," he promised, urging her down the steps of the veranda. A limo waited in the shade of a magnolia tree.

"I have my car," Suzanne protested when she realized his intent.

"Only for a moment. If you'll give me your keys, Sam will take it to wherever you wish. I'll see that you and it are reunited after we eat." Another man got out of the car at their approach.

Suzanne assessed the situation. "You've gone to a lot of trouble," she murmured. "Were you that sure I'd agree?" The idea wasn't a pleasant one.

"Not certain, hopeful. And if you did agree, I didn't want to waste time ferrying around cars or fighting traffic when I could be talking to you. Hence the flashy entourage." He grinned, looking younger and less intimidating. "I really prefer to drive myself."

Suzanne fought being charmed. Smiling, she conceded defeat. The sun was shining. The flower-scented breeze was soft on her skin. She found she didn't want to return to the shop. Darin could handle it, so why not enjoy herself?

"What about this?" She glanced at the box she carried that held the horse carving.

"I would trust Sam with it. He'll take it to the shop for you, and you can call Darin from the car." He waited. This wasn't a woman to be rushed. He had won enough from her for now.

"How do you know Darin?"

"How do you think I knew where to find you?"

She was slipping. Three years ago she would have realized how he had found her. She wasn't sure whether to be glad or sorry that the alertness she had perfected for so long was slowly leaving her. Although she no longer needed it, it was like losing a part of herself.

James wondered at the look in her eyes, seeing secrets and haunted shadows that were unexpected in the woman she seemed to be. He touched her cheek with the back of his hand.

Suzanne looked at him for a moment. "Can I trust you?"

A strange question. "You'd be surprised just how far."

"All right." She stepped back so that his hand fell away. Immediately she missed the warmth of his touch. Tucking the feeling of regret in the back of her mind, she slipped into the limo. The rich scent of leather wasn't a new sensation. The feeling of being crowded was. With James sitting so close to her but not touching, she felt as if her last bit of space was being slowly drawn from her grasp. He leaned forward to hand her the phone.

"Shall I get you a drink while you make your call?"

She nodded while listening to the phone ring at the shop. She was aware of James watching her as she spoke to her assistant. Her eyes were drawn to his. She saw a look of such intensity in his expression that for an instant she lost the thread of the conversation with Darin.

"Suzanne?" Darin sighed. "I think he found you," he muttered, not expecting her to hear him.

Suzanne dragged her gaze from James just as Darin's remark penetrated. She frowned. "I won't ask you to repeat that," she said with an explicit warning. "Just watch for Sam and put the horse in the safe in my office. I'll be back when you see me." In some businesses her last comment might have been an unusual one. But in Suzanne's, Darin was accustomed to the phrase. If Suzanne had a weak point in her construction of a new life, it was this need to move about without the hampering of a time schedule.

"I like that last part," James said as she hung up and accepted a glass of white wine.

She shrugged lightly. "Where are we going?"

"A bit late to ask that."

"Not necessarily. You aren't the type to choose to do something that won't please the woman you're with. Experience shows. Finesse. Planning. A campaign. I can't help asking myself why."

He studied her as she leaned back in the seat and crossed her legs. Beautiful hardly described her. While another woman might have preened and posed, Suzanne did nothing to attract. She was dressed in the height of fashion, a silk suit to match her eyes, small diamond studs in her ears. Deliciously high heels to show off her long legs. Everything about her was ultrafeminine and yet completely businesslike. Her perfume was little more than a promise of scent on the breeze. It touched without lingering. If he leaned an inch closer, he could inhale the fragrance. He wanted to lean that inch closer. More than that, he wanted to pull her into his arms and forget how carefully he intended to bring her to his bed.

Then her words slipped into his thoughts. There was nothing relaxed about him now. "What do you mean, why?" he demanded.

She glanced at him out of the corner of her eye without replying. She continued to sip her wine and pretend that her nerves weren't tightening with each mile that slid by. She still didn't know all the reasons why she had gotten into the car, why she had agreed to this lunch.

"Answer me," he asked once more for a response.

"No." She faced him fully then. "You answer me. I'm fairly well known in this town. You're a man who leaves nothing to chance." She paused.

He waited.

"I don't have affairs." She waited for a denial, an explanation.

"I don't recall asking you for one."

Neither moved. The limo drove on.

"A friend?" Her brows rose, questioning his sanity.

"Isn't it possible?"

She looked at him, allowing her own reaction to show for a moment. "You tell me," she commanded. Lifting her eyes, she made no attempt to hide her attraction to him. Had she not been sure of herself, she would have been giving him a weapon to use against her.

James inhaled sharply at the desire in her eyes. "Damn you," he whispered. "You can't do that."

She smiled. In a blink there was no longer anything to read in her eyes. They were as cool as the first day of winter. There were many in her past who would have recognized that particular gesture. "How do you know I'm not already damned?" She lifted her glass and touched its rim to his. Two swallows finished the excellent vintage.

James drained his glass, setting it aside. "Careful plans be hanged." He took her glass and placed it beside his. In a swift yet seemingly unhurried move, he pulled her into his lap, ignoring her gasp of surprise. The stiffening of her body met a similar fate.

"I won't—"

The rest of her objection was lost in his mouth as it covered hers. Expecting urgency, she found gentleness. Braced to repel, she melted. Wanting control, she lost the edge. Needing space, she found intimacy... sweetness... softness. The dark places in her heart grew light for a moment. The tension uncoiled. Her senses sang a song they had never heard.

James feasted on her lips. Her scent surrounded him. Her body moved against his with such suppleness he felt wrapped in woman. The sensation was decidedly erotic. His desire spiraled to the edge of restraint. He tore his mouth from hers, his breath coming heavily. He stared into her eyes, losing himself in their cloudy depths. Tracing the outline of her lips with his thumb, he waited for her to speak.

When she didn't try to pull away or demand an apology, he said, "I didn't mean to do that."

"For an unplanned act, you did a very thorough job," she responded, finding why she had come with him in his arms. His passion was deep and compelling, but she hadn't lost complete control and neither had he. They had skirted the edge together.

Safety was an odd need to have, but it was one that ruled her life. She had no doubt James could burn out of control. He'd taken her by surprise, but he had really asked her no more than what the image he held of her would call for. He either had not recognized her other self or was ignoring it.

"Do you pounce often?"

He frowned slightly, feeling a flicker of something undefined but insistent. Then she moved against him, and he lost the sensation in the feel of her body.

"With you, I think it could become a habit."

She smiled, relaxing against him for a moment. "And if I pounce?"

"You're not the type. I think that's one of the reasons you intrigue me so. In many ways I'm not quite sure what's going on in that mind of yours."

"You don't know me very well," she pointed out.

She meant her words in more ways than he would ever know. After being careful for so long, it was a delight to drop her guard even a little. James saw only the person she was now. He responded to that person, wanting that person, perhaps liking her a little in the bargain with more than she had hoped, but with less than a force of emotion she had feared could one day be her undoing.

"I want to."

The limo pulled to a stop beside a small lake. Trees dipped slender branches into the water along the bank. Wildflowers blanketed the clearing in gold and violet.

"But first we eat." James tucked her at his side before opening the door to get out. He helped Suzanne from the car as the chauffeur went ahead and spread a quilt on the ground. A wicker picnic basket and satin-covered pillows turned the scene into an idyllic invitation. Impressed and charmed, Suzanne watched the preparations.

"All I need is a parasol."

He laughed softly and signaled to the other man. In moments a dainty, lacy confection was handed to James. "You command. I provide," he teased, opening the frilly umbrella.

Suzanne was vaguely aware of the limo being driven away, leaving her and James alone. "You are—"

He touched a finger to her lips as he lifted the parasol over her head, shading them both. "Don't tell me. Just enjoy this time...with me." He was flirting now. His lips traced the path of his finger. Her breath was a sweet sigh he savored. His arm slipped about her waist, drawing her closer. "Just tell me you aren't sorry you came."

"I'm not," she admitted. She eased away from him, a little surprised when he let her go. For a split second his arms had tightened. Her fingers closed around the umbrella handle, encircling his. "It's been years since I've been on a picnic, and no one has ever given me a parasol before.'"

He laughed softly. "I like being original." He tucked her arm in his. "Besides, you aren't an ordinary woman." He missed her sharp glance as he picked his way across the slightly uneven ground. "You remind me of someone who has stepped out of another time."

He sounded so convinced, she almost told him then. She was living a lie, a lie he believed. He didn't see the woman she really was. He wanted the illusion she had created out of nothing. He never would have bought

her such an impossibly frilly nothing if he had known
her before. For the first time, the deception she had
learned to live so perfectly seemed wrong. What would
it have been like if they could have met on equal
ground? Would he have wanted her then? He would
never had handled her as if she were fragile. He might
have brought her on a picnic, but it probably wouldn't
have been this elegant little rendevous. He would have
walked at her side, not watched the ground to help her
over the rough spots. Which did she really prefer? And
was she suddenly wondering about her life for him or
for herself? Or had she been cautious for so long that
she was beginning to feel the pinch of the restrictions
on her? Of all the questions, the last was the one she
wanted to believe the most. It would be the easiest
solved.

Four

So tell me about yourself. Where you went to school. Who your friends were. How you got into the import-export business." James watched her face as she twirled the parasol over her head. The pale green ribbons and lace rippled with each circle, casting interesting shadows over her skin. He thought about the impulse that had made him stop at the boutique and purchase the frilly bit of nothing. Romantic gestures weren't his normal style, yet he found this one right. Suzanne was made for spoiling, for treating gently.

"Time to sing for my supper?"

He smiled at her. Her voice was rich, slow and smooth, pleasing to his ear. The slight tension of his workday lessened at the easy cadences. He relaxed, leaning back on his elbow to watch her. "I did provide a morsel or two."

She laughed. "Pâté. Caviar. Champagne. Strawberries. Whipped cream. Cheese. It's a wonder I'll be able to walk after your idea of a picnic."

"You didn't like it?"

"What woman wouldn't?"

He liked the small thrusts and parries of their conversation. They had enough spice to appeal without stinging. "Is that the only reason?"

The teasing mood vanished for both of them. The parasol stopped twirling. "No," she answered slowly. The look in his eyes was warm, sincere. She responded to it as much as to the man. One lie between them was enough.

He sighed before reaching for her. He had meant to wait but found he couldn't. She was more than he had expected, all the traits of a woman he could admire and desire rolled into one exquisite package. She came to him, the umbrella dropping to the blanket unnoticed. "Do you have any idea how much I want you?"

She knew he didn't expect an answer.

"I want to bury myself in your gentleness. I want to feel you in my arms. I want to hear your soft voice in the darkness of the night." He laughed a little at his flights of fancy. "I sound like a poet."

Suzanne laid her head against his shoulder, feeling like a fraud even as an unbearable sweetness unfurled within her. She wasn't sweet or soft or gentle or any of those things he thought her. But she wanted to be—for herself, for him. She wanted the beauty that surrounded her this moment to be real beyond the moment. James desired her. Her body felt it, her mind knew it. Yet it was the aura of innocence, of peace and sunlight in the day he had planned for her, that drew her to his arms.

"You'd be disappointed." How did she tell an incredibly sexy man that it was more than the desire for his body that burned in her veins and made her ache for more closeness? How did she explain that she needed what he was offering her more than he could know? Honor demanded she give him as much warning as she could. The past had made many things of her, but she'd never been a cheat or a user.

He placed a finger under her chin and lifted her head. "Let me be the judge of that. Come out with me. I won't rush you. Take your time and get to know me. Stop running."

"I thought I had," she whispered. How could he give her time when even now she could feel the tension of need unfulfilled in his body? His control was beyond her comprehension. Had he been a part of the shadows she knew so well, she would have feared him as she had feared no other. James could have been either an unbeatable friend or unstoppable enemy.

"A little, perhaps. But not completely." He watched her eyes. They, more than her expression, gave away her thoughts. Her lashes flickered. He felt the faint softening in her limbs. He drew her closer. Wanting to do more than hold her, he settled for what he could get.

"All right. When?" she said softly.

"Tonight. Dinner. Seven."

"I'd like that." So easy to agree. So hard to hold back the emotions building within.

James lowered his head, giving her time to withdraw. She met him halfway. Surprised, he took the lips she offered. If the first kiss had been impulsive, this one wasn't. He used every bit of expertise he knew. He gave her a taste of his passion without seeking to overwhelm or to claim. His restraint was slow torture. His body shouted for release. He denied himself for the response she gave.

"We should be getting back," Suzanne whispered, fighting the instincts of her body to give in to the white-hot heat of desire. James wouldn't understand the intensity. He didn't know this woman could burn, and she wasn't going to show him, despite the fact she wanted him badly.

James's arms tightened then slowly eased. He had promised to give her time. His word was hurting in ways he hadn't anticipated, but he would keep it. "I suppose." He tried for a smile as he withdrew completely to get to his feet. Reaching down, he offered Suzanne a hand.

"The sooner I get you back, the sooner we can go out."

She laughed softly, relieved that the desire was ebbing, that her composure was holding. She had been worried for a moment. "You are a very *A*-to-*Z* thinker. I like that."

James gathered the quilt while she finished putting the dishes in the basket. "I thought women preferred emotion to logic."

"I hear a touch of male peeking out with that remark."

"Not a bit of it." He handed her the parasol. "Frankly, I think my sex got the short end of the stick. Emotion can be a very strong motivating force. Anger, for instance, can push a person past his own strength. Fear can turn brave people into cowards or cowards into heroes. Logic won't do that."

Suzanne agreed, but it would hardly be keeping in character to say so. "But it can also deceive someone into making wrong decisions."

He shrugged, the sunlight trapped briefly in his dark brown hair. "Two sides to every coin." He glanced down the narrow road. A thin cloud of dust signaled the returning limo. "Right on time."

"It would surprise me if he were anything else," Suzanne said without thinking.

James turned to her in surprise. "Do I strike you as a tough employer?"

"No, of course not." Suzanne thought fast. There was only one drawback in playing a role. You had to keep your guard up, the mask in place. Just for an instant, she had forgotten and painted herself into a corner. "You impress me as a man who asks of others exactly what he gives of himself. You aren't perfect, but you work at it without being obsessive about it."

The car pulled to a stop beside them. Suzanne concealed a small sigh of relief. Benny would have had her head on a platter for such a stupid slip. She wasn't supposed to be that perceptive. She was an ordinary woman, a little soft, a little smart professionally, but nothing sharp. She had no angles, no surprises, no flashes of intuition. She had created her persona out of traits directly opposed to her own. She had no ex-

cuse for blowing her cover. Or did she, she wondered
as her normal coordination deserted her when James
took her arm. Perhaps desire had more to answer for
than she had given it credit.

Caught in her thoughts, she stumbled a little over
the rough ground. Sharply honed reflexes almost
saved her, but at the last second she remembered her
role and let James catch her. Guilt at her tactics
pricked her conscience even as she softened against
him.

James held her close, liking the way she leaned on
him. She was all woman in his arms—soft, sexy and
too desirable for his resolutions. "Woman, I wish you
were someone I could sweep off her feet," he muttered, not meaning for her to hear.

Suzanne heard but pretended not to. He couldn't
know his wish was echoed in her mind. "I'm sorry.
These heels aren't made for this."

James was not a man to resist an opening like that.
With a smooth move, James lifted her into his arms
and carried her the few feet to the car.

Suzanne froze. No man had ever treated her so gal-
lantly. In her world, both past and present, she stood
alone. "I didn't mean . . ." she protested.

James silenced her with a look. "Do you ever wish
we weren't so modern? Do you ever wish you could go
back to the days when men were chivalrous and
women were soft creatures to be taken care of?"

She shook her head even as the idea took hold.

"I'll tell you a secret that I've never told anyone. I
do. Oh, I don't want to put women in a subservient
place or make myself into a master type. But I like

being able to pick you up without worrying if I'm stepping on your rights as a person. I like holding you. I like buying that parasol. It's pretty. And you look good enough to eat, sitting in the shade of it with those ribbons blowing in the breeze. We've lost things like that with all this equality stuff. Oh, I know we gained a lot." He shook his head, glancing up as the chauffeur finished putting the picnic things in the trunk and opened the door for them. "Forget it. I'm rambling." He covered the distance to the car without looking at her again. He couldn't think what had gotten into him. This afternoon was holding more surprises than he had anticipated.

Suzanne slipped across the seat to make room for him beside her. His face was a study in what she suspected was self-directed anger, regret and confusion. The emotions sharpened the cut of his features, creating a ruthless cast that was new. She shivered, realizing she was looking at the man who had carved a mini-empire in the business world.

"I like those little touches," she murmured, wanting the charming companion back. "I get tired of being alone and strong." The words were unplanned, not a part of the role. The truth in them shocked her. She paused, stunned. Until now, she couldn't remember one time in her life when she had wanted someone to lean on. Even when she had learned Benny had been killed on their last mission together, she hadn't looked for or wanted a shoulder to cry on.

"Suzanne, what is it?" James touched her cheek, watching her closely. She looked so lost. Every protective instinct went on alert. He wanted to pull her into his arms and shelter her from whatever had caused the change.

Suzanne blinked, forcing the memories away. She made herself smile. Would she ever forget? "I'm fine. I was wandering in the past. Thinking about what you had said."

Amazed at the disappointment he felt that she wouldn't confide in him, James sat back. "I shouldn't have asked. After all, we don't know each other well enough to exchange confidences."

The car angled onto the highway to take them back to the city. Suzanne let the swing of the turn ease her closer to James. Her breast brushed his arm. He tensed and glanced at her.

"I didn't lie to you," she murmured softly, wanting to take the sting from her evasion away.

"I didn't say you did."

"You thought it."

"Perhaps." He shrugged. "It doesn't matter." But it did, and he didn't understand why.

She touched his hand. She knew she should let the matter drop but couldn't. She had hurt him. "It does to me."

The sudden husky depth to her voice startled him. The pleading look in her eyes added a significance to her comment that escaped him but one that he wanted to understand. "Why?"

"I don't like lies. I've had to tell a few in my time, but I don't like them."

There was a wealth of emotion tied up in the simple statements. Just for a moment James wondered if Suzanne was really the woman he thought her. The

Suzanne who had smiled at him from the shade of the parasol was an opal with gentle swirls of colors, rounded contours. This one was the flash and brilliance of a diamond. The angles were crystal clear, not cold, not hard, yet stronger than any substance he had encountered. Her lashes lowered, and, when she looked at him again, he knew it had only been a trick of the light. Her body was soft against his, her fragrance intoxicating.

"I don't like lies, either. I, too, have used them. My world sometimes seems built on half-truths, evasions and dissembling." He bent his head to brush her lips, holding himself in check. Slowly. The word was etched in his mind. He wanted her badly. More, with every moment he spent with her. She was his fantasy come to life. "Seven seems like years away."

Suzanne collapsed on the couch. She wasn't tired, but she felt drained of energy, oddly off balance. After quitting the government service, she had been so sure of her course, so positive it was the only way she would have a chance at a normal life.

The life-style and background she had created for herself had been a nice blend of truth and fiction. The loss of Benny had made her determined not to allow herself to ever again be drawn into a situation where her presence spelled danger for a friend or lover. Suzanne Frazier, import-export dealer, had been born from her real name, her real hobby. She used her own money, saved out of the very generous salary Uncle Sam offered to those who risked life and limb in its service. New Orleans had been her birthplace and home for exactly the first three days of her life. Her parents were dead. She had no brothers, no sisters. No one to take or leave behind when she had cut the ties with her old home in Washington.

She had come to New Orleans, bought the house she shared now with her tenant, set up her business and gotten on with the life she had decided she wanted. She had learned not to jump at shadows. She had formed friendships. She had begun to live in the daylight and sleep when it was dark. There were no more hurried calls in the middle of the night. No flights to strange places. No pouches of sensitive merchandise to transfer. No codes. No secrets. No people waiting for that one misstep. No looking over her shoulder. No living on the edge of danger, so high that nothing could compare with the surge of excitement of the hunt, the chase or the outwitting of the hunter. She ate regular meals consisting of foods she recognized.

And she slept alone. The one thing that had not changed. Benny had been her friend, her mentor, and the man who had trained her to be the highly efficient courier of top-secret information that she had been. But he had never been her lover. They were too close for that. He'd understood her too well.

She had been content with her life—until James. She should have been glad that the illusion she had created for herself was all he saw. He was offering her all that she wanted, without poking into the Pandora's box of her past.

"But it's a lie, damn it," she muttered in despair. The one thing she had not considered, not allowed for, was that she would meet a man like James. It hadn't occurred to her that she could be hurt, when the one she was attracted to saw only the image of the woman she portrayed and not the reality beneath it. But she wanted him too much to back away from the hurt that might lie in the future. That realization gave her the energy to shower and change. James would return soon. She didn't want to keep him waiting.

Suzanne twisted in front of the mirror. The soft swish of the silk against her legs was the only sound in the room. Matte black. Pearls. She had meant to be conservative and restrained. She had succeeded in being elegant and dramatic. The fluid cut of her gown skimmed her breasts and hips, only hinting at the fullness it touched. The flared skirt flirted with her stocking-clad knees and danced above slender black heels. The pearls had come from Japan. The diamonds in the clasp and the earrings were from South Africa. The silk was a gift from a Chinese merchant for whom she had done a service. Her lingerie was French, her shoes, Italian.

"I'm a walking United Nations, and I've never been nervous in my life but I am tonight." She lifted her hands and studied her quivering fingers.

The doorbell rang. She started. Taking a deep breath, she went to let James into her apartment and her life.

James stared at her as she stood silhouetted in the doorway. He had known she was beautiful. He hadn't realized she could take his breath away. From the top of the vivid red hair to the impossibly high heels she wore, she was more woman than he had ever known.

"You did the impossible," he whispered, stepping forward to take her in his arms. Every good intention went out the window. "You turned beautiful into extraordinary." He took her lips, savoring her soft sigh of pleasure as she melted against him. He explored her mouth, deepening the kiss as he stroked her back, urging her closer.

Suzanne let him lead the way. She wanted everything he had to offer the way he offered it. She wanted to know his brand of loving. She wanted to come to him without another's knowledge of the way she moved with James. She couldn't offer him the first time for her body, but she suddenly realized she wanted to offer him the first time for her mind. So she waited, following when she easily could have met passion with passion. She sighed deeply when he lifted his head.

"If we don't go now, I won't let you go."

"Is that so bad?" She loved the sound of his voice.

"Not for me. But it might be for you." He looked down the hall to the darkened bedroom.

Suzanne glanced over her shoulder. The temptation was great. For one moment she almost gave in. Then she glanced back at him and saw in his eyes what he expected her to do. He was already accepting her refusal. But soon, she promised herself.

"Perhaps you're right," she murmured.

He kissed her quickly before putting her away from him with a faint smile. "I wish I weren't." He looked around. "Where's your wrap?"

"I'll get it." Suzanne turned away, heading for the bedroom. She needed a moment to regain her composure. James had the knack of unraveling her without seeming to try.

He was standing by the windows when she returned. Turning, he smiled. "I like your apartment. You have quite a collection of beautiful things." He came to her, taking her lace jacket and holding it for her.

"I travel a lot. Always have." There was no point in hiding that part of her past. It had a way of cropping up without warning.

"Was that why you decided to go into the import-export line?" He urged her to the door, pausing for her to lock up.

"Partly. But most of the reason is I like the unusual. Cultures, history, people, they all interest me."

This time James helped her into a Testarossa Ferrari. The low-slung lines were highly prized in the automotive world, some owners waiting as long as six months to get one of the rare cars from the factory.

"You believe in the unusual, yourself," she remarked, appreciating the well-mannered growl of the sports car's motor.

He grinned. "When you don't have anyone but yourself depending on your salary, you can afford to be a little self-indulgent."

She leaned back to enjoy the ride. The kiss might never have happened if it hadn't been for the lingering remnants of desire she saw in his eyes. Her own body throbbed with life and need. She ignored both his response and her own. The night stretched before them.

"So tell me about yourself," she insisted.

"What do you want to know?"

She laughed softly, suddenly feeling young and free again. "Anything. Everything. You know a lot about me. Return the favor."

He laughed at her command. "That soft voice of yours doesn't do orders very well," he said. "But I'll give you what you want anyway."

Suzanne didn't rise to the provocative remark.

"I'm thirty-four. Never been married. Never had time. No trauma in my past. No women ready to scalp me for being less than fair. I decided I wanted to be wealthy, sometime in my freshman year at high school. We had this kid, Biff, whose father owned the biggest hotel in the county. That brat was always lording it over the rest of us for what we didn't have. I got fed up with him one day. I couldn't punch the twerp out, because I was bigger than he was and my dad was rabid on the subject of a man using his strength against smaller rivals. I decided the only way to beat Biff was to get richer than he was. I made it. Not that it mattered much by the time I did. I'd met a lot of Biffs by then. Learned a bit about myself, too. Money stopped being a goal and became a kind of tally sheet. I guess you could say I got hooked on the challenge of beating the odds. The larger my corporation gets, the more I want it to grow. Work is more than the word implies. I like the thrust and parry of the business arena. My competitors would tell you I thrive on opposition."

"Do you?"

He glanced at her, taking the opportunity afforded by a red light to study her. "Yes. My life is just the way

I like it. The only thing I'm missing is someone special to share it with. The thing is finding her."

Suzanne watched him as carefully as he did her. "What do you want?"

The light changed. James muttered an oath before easing the car forward. "Better timing."

Five

You asked me earlier what I would like." James sat back, gazing at Suzanne across the candlelit table. Violins played softly in the background. He had chosen the most romantic restaurant in town for their first real date. The evening was turning out exactly as planned. Suzanne fit the atmosphere to perfection. She spoke French like a native Parisian. She listened when he spoke, asking sharp, concise questions. He had told her more in the past two hours than he had confided to all but his most trusted friends. He was more relaxed and yet more curiously alive than he had been in as long as he could remember. The stress of the day, the irritants, the highs, the lows seemed far removed from the reality of this moment.

Suzanne waited, at ease but alert. She had known

James had not forgotten her question. She had expected him to bring it up before now.

"I lead a hectic life by choice. Lately, I've been considering my future."

Suzanne managed to conceal her surprise at his honesty. She hadn't anticipated this turn to the conversation.

"Not many women would put up with what I do. I'm gone more often than I'm home. And when I am home I use the time to relax, to recharge for the next day. Women today want a career. They should have it, too. So how would I handle a working woman who in all probability would come home as tired as I and as ready to unwind? I don't think I want to go through a series of relationships hunting for the right partner."

"Sounds to me as if the thinking you're doing is going to save you a lot of heartache in the end," she replied, striving for a neutral tone while her mind worked fast.

"Perhaps. Do you think a woman could be happy in the kind of life I lead?" He had never believed in dodging an important issue. Now that he had started this line, he had to finish. Her response would help him decide what to do next.

Suzanne lifted her glass, staring at the contents for a moment. "If she loved you." She raised her eyes to his. A loaded question deserved a loaded answer.

He studied her for a moment. So she still believed in love. It was odd, but he hadn't thought she would. Despite the softness that was so apparent, he felt a kind of realism about her that precluded the nebulous concept of love. He frowned a little at the realization.

Actually, given what he knew of her, the reverse should have been true.

"It's funny, but I'm not sure I believe in that commodity. Too many people spout words of love and two or three years later haul themselves off to divorce court, hating their spouse."

Their waiter arrived with the dessert trolley, breaking the mood. Suzanne was more relieved than she dared show. Something in James's eyes had worried her for an instant. He had looked at her as though he were really seeing her.

"What will you have?" James glanced without interest over the display.

Needing to prolong the interruption, Suzanne pointed to a lacy white cake on a silver stand. "A piece of the white chocolate froufrou."

The dessert was one of her favorites. A combination of *génoise* brushed with Grand Marnier syrup and sandwiched with white chocolate mousse flavored with candied orange.

James refilled his wineglass, declining to join her. The waiter departed. "I didn't intend to say all that. You shouldn't be so easy to talk to."

Suzanne lifted the first bite to her mouth, completely oblivious to the delicate taste of the sweet. "As are you. Don't worry about it. I know you were really thinking out loud." She hoped. Contemplating having an affair with James was one thing; considering a more permanent liaison was quite another.

James wanted badly to object but held his peace. He had done enough rushing for one night. "Do you have plans for tomorrow?"

"The usual single person's chores."

"I have a boat. I was thinking of taking a slow ride up the Mississippi. Interested?"

Suzanne hesitated. The outing sounded delightful. The summer was already heating up to an uncomfortable degree. "A day on the river would be pleasant."

"I could invite some friends if you like."

She considered taking the out he offered and discarded the thought. Some things had survived her rebirth. She was no coward. "But you don't want to," she pointed out, smiling a little.

"No, I don't," he admitted frankly. "But if it is the only way I can get you to come out with me, then I will suffer through it."

"And if I say, no, either way."

He studied her and shook his head. "I hope it isn't arrogance on my part which tells me you won't do that."

She laughed then. It was impossible not to. He challenged. He retreated. He teased then caught her off guard with his probing questions and sharp looks. She should have run a mile, but she was going to walk with him instead. A fool's chance. A woman's need. "I think you are a dangerous man, James Southerland. You turn on that charm at just the right moment."

"Never give your weakness away to the opponent." He reached across the table and took her hand in his. "I might just turn it to my advantage."

"And what would your daddy say to that? Or didn't his philosophy apply to a man-woman situation." She tipped her head, considering him. Teasing a man had never been her game. Tonight she found it was the only way to play.

"You know you aren't at all what you seem." His interest sharpened as the flash of surprise in her eyes glowed clearly for a moment. "I think I should have paid closer attention to that glorious red hair of yours. I may use my charm as you call it to get my way, but, honey, you have softness and the velvet glove down to an art form."

Suzanne pushed away her half-eaten dessert. She couldn't swallow another bite. James, if he but knew it, had hit close to the bone.

"Are you implying I have a temper?" She deliberately misunderstood him.

The disappointment in his eyes was faint. Suzanne wished she dared continue meeting his challenge.

James caught himself on a sigh. He was a fool. Just for a moment she had seemed different. Her voice had lost its lazy draw. While it hadn't lost its softness, it had become more decisive. For a second she had been a woman who thrived on challenges, a woman who would dare anything. He didn't understand the dichotomy.

"Forget it. Put it down to a tired businessman not making any sense." James gestured toward her plate. "Are you finished? Shall we go?"

Suzanne nodded before getting to her feet. "It is getting late." She felt his withdrawal and his confusion, although he masked it well.

The drive to her home was short and mostly silent. Other than to ask after her comfort, James said nothing. "I won't come in," he said as she unlocked the door.

Suzanne turned to face him, her eyes searching his. He leaned against the door, watching her. "I enjoyed myself," she whispered.

"So did I." The hands he had jammed into his pockets clenched with the need to pull her into his arms. "How early can you be ready tomorrow?"

"Seven? Or is that too soon?"

"It's fine." He wanted to kiss her, to bury himself in her arms until she wanted nothing nor anyone as much as she wanted him. He didn't dare touch her. His need was too great. His control was slipping.

Suzanne stepped forward, knowing she was playing with fire but unable to help herself.

He caught her shoulders, holding her away from his body. "Don't."

"Why not?"

"I won't be able to stop."

Her hands settled on his chest. She could feel the beat of his heart beneath her palm. The warmth of skin burned through the fabric of his shirt. The scent of male wrapped around her, weighting her lashes.

"It's crazy, but I don't want you to."

James fought his resolution, his instincts. His fingers tightened, and, without realizing it, he drew her to lean against him. Her body fit his in a way no woman's had before. Her head was tipped over his arm, her eyes half-closed, drowsy with desire.

"You want me," James whispered.

"I know. You want me, too."

"I can't. I don't want you to regret this in the morning."

"Don't talk. Feel. Does it feel as if I'll regret anything in the morning?" She brushed her breasts against his chest. The friction of fabric on fabric was highly erotic. Her gasp of pleasure echoed his deeper one.

"Be sure."

"I am."

His mouth took the words from her lips. His hands molded her to him, arching her hips into the source of the hard ache and driving him to the limits of his restraint. Without breaking the kiss, he lifted her into his arms and walked into her home, shutting the world outside away. The lights were on. He hardly noticed as he found her bedroom. Her scent was everywhere, a living thing to tease him with promises of what was to come. He set her on her feet, letting her body slide down his in a slow torturous descent. They were both breathing heavily when she stood before him. Two clips secured her hair. He pulled them out so the red cloud could tumble free. The pearls were next. The zipper at the back of her dress whispered silently down until the gown fell off her shoulders, lingering for a tantalizing instant on the tips of the silk-and-lace-cloaked breasts. He lifted her free of the black pool of silk at her feet.

"You're beautiful," he said softly.

"So are you." Suzanne watched him as he undressed her, knowing that this first time was his choice. She wanted to be special and all the things she had dreamed of. She wanted what she had forgotten had existed—innocence, passion, warmth and giving.

The slip was next. A wisp of a bra, and her breasts were bare. Proud, the tips pouted in rosy perfection against the creamy white fullness. A garter belt, lacy and black as midnight, secured her stockings. Bikini panties rose high on her thighs to tip in a low V across her abdomen.

"I almost hate to take off these pretty things," he whispered, gently pulling on the lace-covered elastic garters. His lips teased one nipple then the other.

Suzanne moaned deep in her throat. She didn't care what he left on or took off as long as he didn't stop.

James slipped his fingers beneath the edge of the panties and slid them down her long legs. His hand trailed up the inside of her thighs, lingering at but not probing the russet curls at the juncture. Suzanne arched against the weight of his touch. An unbearable ache was building and only he could assuage it.

James eased her back until her knees pressed against the bed. Taking her weight, he lowered them to the mattress. Her hips cradled his. Soon he would fill her, but not yet. He wanted to know her, know what pleased her, what excited her.

"Easy, honey," he whispered when she pulled at his shirt. "Not yet."

"I want you." Suzanne pulled his head down, taking his mouth as he had taken hers. "Stop teasing."

"Not teasing. Pleasuring us both." His hand swept down until he found the center of her softness. Her gasp sent need spiraling through him. His fingers moved and she cried out again. He held her as the shudders built. And when she bent tight across his arm, he covered her lips, swallowing her moan of release.

Suzanne quivered in the aftermath. His arms were a cradle of warmth, his eyes hot and possessive as he gazed down at her. She had never felt more vulnerable in her life. "I never—"

He touched her lips, silencing her words. "I know."

"But you didn't—"

He smiled. "I know that, too. But I will. If you still want me."

She smiled, as well. The vulnerability crept away as she lay there looking at him. She had pleased him with her response. If he had shouted it, she couldn't have been more sure.

"You have too many clothes on."

"So I do." James slipped one arm free to shrug out of his jacket. Suzanne started to raise up to help him. He stopped her with a shake of his head. "Let me. I'm quicker."

She leaned back and watched him. Even when he moved completely away from her to shed his pants and shirt, she still watched. His eyes never left hers. When he came back to her, she opened her arms to receive him.

James lifted Suzanne into his arms. His lips moved over her face, caressing all the curves and hollows that he had already made his own. When his mouth brushed over hers, Suzanne moaned and threaded her fingers through his hair. Her lips opened, wanting him, needing him, hungry for the sensual excitement of his mouth. James's tongue slid between her teeth, thrusting slowly across her tongue, retreating, thrusting again, inciting her with the love rhythm. She pulled him closer, pressing her aching breasts against his chest. Hard nipples buried in the dark hair sent a sweet pain spiraling through and brought a moan of pleasure to James's throat. Without ending the slow movements of his tongue, James moved his fingers down Suzanne's spine, probing at the base until he found the sensitive hollow that made her cry out and arch to him.

Eyes closed, Suzanne felt herself come undone all over again, slow liquid rhythms uncoiling deep in her body. She shivered and sighed and melted against James, knowing only his touch. She kissed his shoulders and the muscles bunched in his arms. She felt the shiver of his response. She continued moving her lips and teeth and tongue across his chest, glorying in his muted groan.

James drank deeply of her mouth. His control was almost gone. The blind seeking of her body for his was his undoing. Suzanne was all woman in his arms. He slipped his knee between her thighs, urging them apart. Raising himself above her, he entered slowly, savoring every inch of flesh he claimed.

Suzanne twisted beneath him, adjusting to the weight of his body and to his length filling her. His hand stroked down until he found the liquid heat of her. A single touch sent tiny passionate convulsions rippling through her.

"Now, James," she cried, pushing against him with all her strength.

"Slowly," he whispered against her lips as his hot flesh moved over her in a long inflaming slide. Sweat broke out on his body at the demands he placed on it. He didn't care. He wanted to know every movement, to feel every quiver. Suzanne matched him thrust for thrust. Nature and desire took over. His control broke. With a cry he buried himself deep in her warmth, spilling out the essence of his body.

Suzanne arched, giving and taking all in the same instant. Quivering, tears pouring from her eyes from the force of her release, she lay beneath him, wrapped in his warmth and the scent of their joining.

For slow sweet minutes, they lay in each other's arms, drifting back to an awareness of the present. James pressed his lips against the tangled fall of red hair. He kissed her temple, her cheek, the inner curve of her ear, the corners of her smile. Her finger moved down his back to the muscles of his buttocks and beyond. James groaned and tightened inside her, sending sensations flashing through her. Her skin was still sensitive to the smallest touch. Her hands glided over his body, exploring, learning.

"Much as I like that, we're going to be in trouble if you don't stop," James warned huskily. He moved deeply inside her, silently showing her just what he meant. Her hips kept rhythm with his. "Is this what you want?" Her need surprised him. He knew he had satisfied her.

"If you do." While the fire still burned for her, she would demand nothing beyond what he could give.

Suzanne meant one thing, James heard another. "You're the kind of woman men dream about," he breathed against her lips as he arched into her, taking them to the peak of desire in a surge of passion.

Later she slept in his arms. He held her close, needing her warmth as he had no other woman's before her. He awoke first and lay watching her. It was late in the morning. The boat trip they had planned seemed unnecessary now. Instead all he wanted to do was spend the day with her in this bed. He frowned a bit at his thoughts. No, it was more than that. He wanted to see her smile at him, to hear her voice, to simply be with her. He liked her, he realized. The attraction had blinded him to that fact until now. She was the fantasy he had woven for himself, his idea of a perfect woman. She was neither subservient nor aggressive. She matched him in bed, yet she let him take the lead. She was intelligent, warm, sweet-natured and caring. Professionally she was a success. Her business kept her busy, but it didn't seem to rule her life, for she had been willing to take time off for the picnic. She had integrity. She was honest.

His frown became a smile. He had chosen well. He would have to remember to thank his sister for her matchmaking when he saw her next.

Suzanne stretched in her sleep, her hand encountering a warm hard wall of muscle. Her lashes fluttered before opening to stare into James's face. The smile on his lips found its way to hers. "Sleep well?" she murmured. The sun from the open windows poured over the bed, painting his body gold. He looked deliciously sexy and all male.

"Silly question, woman," he answered, bending his head to kiss her. "No regrets?"

82 WOMAN IN THE SHADOWS

"Should there be?"

"Probably. I rushed you." He nuzzled her ear, nipping at the earlobe.

Suzanne arched her neck to give him better access. "I imagine I could have said no and you would have listened." She moved close to him, slipping her arms around his neck.

"I hope I would have." His mouth trailed lower. Her nipples were too great a temptation to resist.

Suzanne sighed in pleasure. "I like the way you begin the day."

"Good."

She threaded her fingers through his hair as the single word rumbled against the skin. The faint stubble of a beard was an erotic rasp across her flesh. Desire uncoiled. She twisted nearer, pulling him on top of her.

James took the hint. Having tasted her passion, he knew he couldn't wait to have her again. With a smooth move he joined their bodies, creating one out of two.

"We never did go on that boat trip," Suzanne said as she stretched lazily.

"Do you mind?"

"I liked the picnic in bed we had instead. But do you have a thing about picnics?"

"Not until I met you I didn't. Now, I could get addicted."

"Addictions aren't good for you."

A kiss. Silence. A moan. "Do you like that?" James asked.

"What do you think?" she replied.

"I think I'm a lucky man."

"There is no such thing as luck." Suzanne pulled him down on her until his whole weight had her pinned to the bed. "You make things happen or you don't."

James lifted his head, smiling despite the desire glittering in his eyes. "That sounds like something I would say. It doesn't sound like you at all."

"You think I'm superstitious?" Once again, she deliberately misunderstood him while silently cursing her slip. For a split second she wished James wasn't quite so sharp.

"I think you are sexy, desirable and wholly feminine." He kissed her deeply. "Now stop talking and start moving. I'm getting hot lying here thinking about what we could be doing."

Six

I swear if I see you come to work with that smile on your face one more day, I'm going to be ill. You'd think a boss would have a little sympathy for her overworked and underpaid assistant."

"Rough weekend, Darin?" Suzanne studied him. "You look like the morning after the night before." She was becoming used to his teasing. He seemed to delight in her new personal life, and, since his interest was completely without malice and wholly supportive, she couldn't make herself deny him his small pleasure.

Darin slumped in the chair across the desk. "Thanks a lot for nothing. I hate Mondays. They had to have been invented by a sadist."

Suzanne laughed.

Darin scowled, pretending irritation. "Since South-erland got in your life, you sure have changed."

Suzanne's light mood darkened. The seriousness of his tone was in variance with his expression. "What do you mean?" She almost didn't ask the question. Her time with James was so free and simple that she didn't want anything to mar the halcyon days.

"You've been with him about three weeks. You smile more. You're..." He hesitated, his hands spreading in a helpless gesture. "I don't know. You talk soft, look soft, but every once in a while you can be sharp, very shrewd, really aloof. In a way, kind of intimidating." He grimaced at the word. "That's not an insult. Really. It's just envy. I guess what I mean is that you're more friendly now."

Startled, Suzanne didn't speak for a moment. Three weeks. Had it been that long? The time had slipped by. She couldn't remember being as happy as she was with James. He was unexpected in so many ways. He treated her as if she were fragile and delicate, yet he didn't overpower her or try to run her life. He simply made them a place between both their lives. He hadn't lied when he said his own schedule was hectic. Even now he was out of town and had been for two days. But he would be back tonight, a day early. That was the reason for her smile. He had called, waking her out of a restless sleep to give her the good news.

"You also tend to go off in a daydream on occa-sion," Darin added meaningfully.

Suzanne came back to the present, ignoring the gentle barb. "Think you can handle the shop to-day?"

Darin tipped his head to one side, grinning. "You know being left here alone is my favorite thing," he reminded her. "It feeds my ego."

She laughed. "Your ego doesn't need feeding. In another few years you're going to blaze a trail in this town and we both know it. So stop grumping and groaning and go earn that exorbitant salary you talked me into giving you."

"You mean that chicken feed you maneuvered me into taking," he returned, pushing to his feet. "Tell Southerland I said hello the next time you see him. And warn him I'm doing more work just so you can play hooky."

Suzanne didn't have a chance to retaliate. Darin whisked himself out the door with a final impudent grin. She laughed a little herself.

"So I'm friendlier now, am I?" She shook her head at his charge.

Darin was proving himself to be even more of an asset, his teasing notwithstanding. It was because she could trust him that she had the freedom to spend more time with James. She sat down marveling at how far she had come. She had thought she had forgotten how to trust anyone. James's influence again. After seeing how he delegated responsibility and still kept a finger on his business pulse, she had given Darin even more freedom in the shop. The results had been well worth the effort. Maybe she should consider making Darin a full partner when the time came. The way he was learning, he would certainly be qualified enough, and money wasn't a problem.

* * *

Suzanne wasn't thinking of Darin when she entered James's town house. The place was neat. The daily maid had been and gone. The refrigerator was well stocked. She stood in front of the master-bedroom closet, surveying the few outfits she had left there. Nothing suited her. If she hadn't had to deal with a last-minute crisis at the shop, she could have taken the time to go home to change. Glaring at the sparse collection, she stepped out of her suit and tossed it over a chair. The slip was next. Then the bra.

James leaned against the door, watching her. She hadn't seen him as yet. He wondered briefly at the frown on her face and forgot it when she began undressing. As always, her movements fascinated him. Maybe it was the result of the t'ai chi she practiced daily, or maybe it was from some hereditary gift. But she was the most graceful woman he had ever seen. Inhaling sharply as the bra slipped from her breasts, he felt the heat pool between his legs.

"You ought to be illegal," he said roughly, coming toward her.

Suzanne swung around, her eyes flashing with pleasure. "How long have you been standing there?"

He stopped before her, his hands reaching up to cup her breasts. "Too long for a man who's been sleeping in a lonely, cold bed for two nights." His thumbs lightly stroked her nipples, bringing them erect.

Suzanne arched against his touch. "You weren't the only one," she whispered, staring at him through half-closed eyes.

"I don't want to go away again like that." He urged her closer. "I hate missing you."

"Ditto."

"Ditto?" James laughed as he lifted her in his arms and carried her to the bed. "Woman, sometimes I think you lie awake nights figuring out ways to torment me."

"I wouldn't do that." Suzanne twisted beneath him, molding her body nearer. "You have on too many clothes."

"I created a wanton. Where are those soft little ways?"

"Gone." The heat in him was more than the hardness pressing against her. It was in the way his hand roved restlessly over her skin. His tension wasn't desire. She sensed it. "What's wrong?"

"Nothing." He bent his head to kiss her.

For the first time in their relationship, she pulled back from him. Now his tension was hers. "Do you want out?" The words hurt her to say. Her one fear grew with each moment of pleasure they shared. Nothing lasted forever. The lesson had been hard learned and unforgettable.

He reared back, his expression stunned. "Does it feel as if I do?" he demanded hoarsely, unable to believe she had uttered, much less thought of, something so impossible.

"No. But something is wrong. Tell me." Threading her fingers through his hair, she searched his eyes. "Is it business?"

"No." He tried to pull his head free, but she was stronger than she looked.

"Then it's me." The ripple of emotion in his body would have gone unnoticed if he hadn't been lying on top of her. "Tell me."

"All right, damn it." He dropped a hard kiss on her lips before rolling so that she was on top, looking down at him. He wanted to see her face, feel her reaction when he made his suggestion.

"I want you to move in with me. Here. I don't like this one-night-here and one-night-at-your-place living we've been doing."

Suzanne stared at him, caught without words. "I thought you were happy with what we had. I got the impression that you preferred no strings. And I know very well that you haven't had women living with you."

"No, I haven't." He had hoped she'd want him as much as he wanted her. He had hoped she'd agree with eagerness, with delight. He felt the disappointment and denied the hurt that lay beneath.

"Then why me?" An affair had been what he had offered, what she had accepted. "I'm no more into ties than you are," she reminded him. Panic rippled across the surface of her mind. She fought to smooth her emotions, to cage the spiraling fear that he would demand more than she could give and force her into leaving.

"Are you saying you don't want to live with me?" Waves of feelings he didn't understand emanated from her, wrapping around him as closely as her arms held him. There was a desperation in her.

"What's wrong with what we have now?"

He wanted to shout at her for not seeing what was so clear to him, but instead he tried to give her lucid reasons. "Being apart is what's wrong. Taking you home so you can get more clothes is what's wrong. Waking up in the middle of the night and not remembering which bedroom I'm in is what's wrong." He shook her once. "Why can't we live together? Neither of us have anyone who would mind." Anger and hurt at her stubbornness bled through every word. "Or is it you don't care enough to want to live with me? Maybe all I am to you is a damn good lover." He arched beneath her, pushing his hips up so that she was fully aware of his arousal. "Good enough to bed but not—"

Suzanne stole his biting words with her lips. The bitterness was unexpected. The pain, too. He resisted her, his mouth closed, his lips sealed. She raised her head, tears she hadn't shed in more years than she could remember in her eyes.

"Damn you! I didn't mean that and you should know it."

"How would I know it? Do you think I haven't felt you withdraw into yourself? Do you think I don't realize how carefully you don't evade my questions about your past but still manage to withhold even the smallest bit of information. I want to know you. More than just this." His hands caressed her breasts. Even in his temper, his touch was made for pleasure. "I'm not asking you for marriage. I'm not demanding the rest of your life."

Pain twisted in her heart. For one insane second she wished he was. Even if she had to deny him, she would have liked to know he wanted her that much. Pure selfishness. Harmless only because it would never become a reality.

"Suzanne!" he prompted when she didn't answer right away.

"I need time." She couldn't bring herself to refuse him completely. "For you, this is easy—"

He laughed, the sound without humor. "I've never done anything half this difficult," he disagreed.

"Your experience is greater than mine. That's all I meant. I need to get used to this." She let the tension flow out of her body. She had to make him believe her even if she couldn't tell him the real reasons why she hesitated. "Time. A little while. I promise."

He watched her in silence for a moment, trying to figure out what she was thinking. Her eyes were dark, her expression too smooth. Her body was still soft, yielding and warm.

"You're doing it again," he said, feeling more defeat than elation at having won a partial agreement.

Suzanne touched his face, smoothing the lines of pain at the corners of his mouth. "It isn't us and our relationship. Take my word for it. Everyone has darkness hidden somewhere in his soul. You keep bumping into mine." She rested her head on his chest, needing to hold him and be held. When his arms closed around her, she was safe. "I'm sorry you see it in me. I wish I could explain."

James laid his cheek against her fiery hair. A hundred questions plagued his mind. He asked none of them, for he knew there would be no answers. Somehow he knew she had given him all she could. "All right. I'll give you time," he whispered. He stroked her bare back, enjoying the texture of her silky skin. "But remember. I haven't forgotten that I asked you," he said softly, nipping at the tender lobe of her ear. She moved against him, increasing the ache of desire.

Suzanne closed her eyes, hurting and wishing more than she had ever in her life. Shadows. Would she ever be able to step out of them completely? No matter how far she ran, how cleverly she hid herself, how carefully she acted, the shadows still lingered to darken the present.

"So, what would you like to do tonight?" James stroked Suzanne's hair back from her face, enjoying the silky feel of the strands wrapping around his fingers. The bedroom was in darkness, neither of them wanting nor needing a light.

Suzanne kissed his shoulder, delighting in the shudder that rippled over him at the caress. "I don't really care. We could call out for something to eat or I can cook. You choose."

James smiled. "I like the way your mind works."

"Is that all you like?"

Startled at the provocative question, James hesitated. "You're getting very sassy," he murmured, his thoughts centering on her body and the way she moved. Food was forgotten. Nothing mattered but holding her, making her his once more.

Suzanne held him off with a hand on his chest. "But I'm starving."

"So am I, but not for food." He pulled her into his arms. Her soft sigh and yielding body made a lie of her protest. "I want you here, now." He searched her face for the smallest sign of refusal. He saw only desire. His need escalated. The ache grew.

"I want you, too. Sometimes, I think too much."

"It can never be too much."

"It can when this burns out." She arched her hips against his.

James frowned at the reminder. "Who says it is going to burn out?" he demanded, his tone revealing another kind of pain.

Suzanne watched him carefully. "No ties, remember?"

"Too well." He shook his head, trying to escape his thoughts.

Panicked at the silken bonds she could feel, Suzanne spoke. "Don't do this. You don't really know me at all. I'm not what you see."

James was in no mood to hear more than the words. "I know you surprise me constantly. I don't mind. I like the flashes of temper beneath that control. I wouldn't want to live with that temperament every day, but your way, it adds spice to our lives. And as for knowing you, I could say the same for myself." He slipped a hand around her nape and drew her lips to his. "We'll find out all we need to know together."

"But James…" Suzanne tried to explain. Now that she had opened Pandora's box, she wanted him to know the whole. The fantasy life she had created for herself was too much of a burden, something she should have realized before their relationship had come this far.

His kiss took the confession from her lips. By the time he raised his head, Suzanne had forgotten what she wanted to say.

"You don't play fair," she whispered, passion lending depth to her voice.

"Needs must . . ." He rolled on his back and pulled her on top of him.

"When the devil drives," she finished for him, her hands glorying in the feel of his skin and the rippling of the muscles beneath her fingers. "I know the feeling." Her fingers tangled in the hair on his chest. She pulled lightly. "Do I ever know the feeling."

He grinned wickedly as he lifted his head to take one erect nipple in his mouth. "I'm glad, lady of mine. Very glad."

"We've had three days together. What do you think?"

Suzanne glanced up from her half of the newspaper. She smiled at James across the breakfast table. "What do I think about what? Eating breakfast? It's okay even if you did use unfair tactics to get me to agree to face an egg at the crack of dawn." She knew what he was asking. They had agreed to spend the whole weekend together. She knew full well he had hoped she'd see how easy it was for them to make a life together. She had. Too clearly. With every hour, the lie became greater, the need to confess stronger, the desire more intense and the wish things could be different unbearable. She had to tell him, but she just couldn't figure out how. So she played, smiled and made love, hoping she would be strong enough to find a way.

"You're mellowing. The last time, yesterday to be exact, you accused me of blackmailing you with my body." He chuckled at her mock glare.

"You have to admit that waiting until I was in a certain position before you brought the subject up was hardly the gentlemanly thing to do."

James aimed for an innocent look but missed. "I was trying to set a slow pace. I thought you liked my slow loving."

Desire, never far from the surface when she was near James, flared to life. Suzanne inhaled deeply, fighting for the control that grew harder to grasp with each day.

James watched her, knowing what she was doing and making no effort to stop her. His body was at war, as well. In a way he and Suzanne were caught in a trap. An intoxicating, wickedly seductive trap of mutual passion. They were restrained people, logical, careful. But when they were together, the rules they lived with seemed false. He touched her and he wanted her. He saw her smile, and he could hear her soft laughter when he held her in the darkness. She looked at him with a long stare, and he knew she was mentally reliving their lovemaking. When her tongue touched her lips, he could taste her mouth and the deep crevice of satisfaction that he could create when they became one.

"Don't look at me like that." Suzanne got up, her movements uncharacteristically jerky.

James frowned at her back. "Is something wrong?"

"No, nothing. I just know the way your mind works." Suzanne poured herself another cup of coffee before turning around to face him. She was back on track. With a look, he could make her forget who she was supposed to be. "We'll be late if we don't get a move on."

James rose and came to her. His hands spanned her waist, his eyes searching hers. "Are you worried about the party this weekend? Would you rather I put this get-together off until you are more comfortable?"

Suzanne met his gaze, fighting the need to tell him just how much she had grown attached to his home. She had expected to feel displaced for a time, but she hadn't. Part of the reason was the way James made a place for her. But too much of the reason was the man himself. No ties. The words were acid etched on her brain right alongside the illusion of Suzanne Frazier. Each day she promised herself she would tell him the truth, and each day she found a dozen reasons to continue the lie. Even now, watching him, knowing he needed her assurance that she was happy with him, she still resisted. She had heard the comment that had started the conversation, but she had chosen to misunderstand it.

Protection? Camouflage? Cowardice? She no longer knew which motivated her. For the first time in

SILHOUETTE® DELIVERS FIRST-CLASS ROMANCE— DIRECT TO YOUR DOOR

Mail the Heart sticker on the postpaid order card today and you'll receive:

—4 new Silhouette Desire® novels—FREE
—a lovely lucite digital clock/calendar—FREE
—and a surprise mystery bonus—FREE

But that's not all. You'll also get:

Money-Saving Home Delivery

When you subscribe to Silhouette Desire®, the excitement, romance and faraway adventures of these novels can be yours for previewing in the convenience of your own home. Every month we'll deliver 6 new books right to your door. If you decide to keep them, they'll be yours for only $2.24* each—that's 26 cents below the cover price, and there is *no* extra charge for postage and handling! There is no obligation to buy— you can cancel at any time simply by writing ''cancel'' on your statement or by returning a shipment of books to us at our cost.

Free Monthly Newsletter

It's the indispensable insider's look at our most popular writers and their upcoming novels. Now you can have a behind-the-scenes look at the fascinating world of Silhouette! It's an added bonus you'll look forward to every month!

Special Extras—FREE

Because our home subscribers are our most valued readers, we'll be sending you additional free gifts from time to time in your monthly book shipments as a token of our appreciation.

OPEN YOUR MAILBOX TO A WORLD OF LOVE AND ROMANCE EACH MONTH. JUST COMPLETE, DETACH AND MAIL YOUR FREE-OFFER CARD TODAY!

*Terms and prices subject to change without notice.

FREE! lucite digital clock/calendar

You'll love your digital clock/calendar!
The changeable month-at-a-glance calendar
pops out and can be replaced with your
favorite photograph. It is yours FREE as
our gift of love!

Silhouette 💕 Desire®

FREE OFFER CARD

4 FREE BOOKS

FREE HOME DELIVERY

PLACE
HEART
STICKER
HERE

FREE DIGITAL CLOCK/CALENDAR

FREE FACT-FILLED NEWSLETTER

FREE MYSTERY BONUS

MORE SURPRISES THROUGHOUT THE YEAR—FREE

☑ **YES!** Please send me four Silhouette Desire®
novels, free, along with my free digital clock/
calendar and my free mystery gift as explained on the
opposite page.

225 CIS JAYV

NAME _____

ADDRESS _____ APT. _____

CITY _____ STATE _____

ZIP CODE _____

Offer limited to one per household and not
valid to current Silhouette Desire®
subscribers. All orders subject
to approval. Terms and prices
subject to change
without notice.

SILHOUETTE "NO RISK" GUARANTEE

• There is no obligation to buy—the free books and gifts remain yours to keep • You receive
books before they're available in stores • You may end your subscription anytime—just write
"cancel" on your statement or return your shipment of books at our cost.

PRINTED IN U.S.A.

Remember! To receive your free books, digital clock/calendar and mystery gift, return the postpaid card below. But don't delay!

DETACH AND MAIL CARD TODAY.

If offer card has been removed, write to:
Silhouette Books, 901 Fuhrmann Blvd., P.O. Box 1867, Buffalo, NY 14269-1867

her life she wasn't sure what she was doing or where she was going.

"Suzanne?" James touched her cheek, drawing her attention. "Where do you go when you hide in your mind?"

She dredged up a faint smile. He was offering her a chance to tell him, but she knew before she spoke she wouldn't take it. "No place important. Sometimes I get lost in this." She waved her hand to encompass their bodies pressed together. "I have to go away to get my bearings. I'm sorry."

"Don't be. I, too, stumble around in the dark. I never knew—" he paused, searching for words he could live with "—caring could be so easy or so hard. I'm not taking too much, am I?" Because he knew the value of his freedom, the need to keep some distance between himself and the world, he recognized the need in her.

"No. But I wonder if I am?" She dropped her head to his shoulder. For a long moment she relaxed against him.

"I tell you what. We'll strike a bargain. If either of us feels the need for more space, we'll tell the other. That should cover all the bases." He waited, wanting a closer relationship but fearing it, too. It was difficult to trust her and himself. He had never felt so vulnerable with a woman.

Suzanne didn't need to consider the suggestion. It was fair. But then James was always fair. "All right." She lifted her head. "And to answer your question about the party. I want to do it. I won't be embarrassed by our living arrangements if that's what you're worried about but won't say. I want to meet your friends."

"Honest?"

The word brought pain. She ignored it. "I just agreed to honesty. I won't go back on my word." Whatever happens in the future, she added silently as she offered her lips for his kiss.

Seven

The phone rang, breaking Suzanne's concentration. She'd been studying the manifest for an order from Denmark. Her eyes still on the papers, she answered with the name of the shop.

"Athena," said a familiar voice.

At the code name that only a very few knew, Suzanne's head came up with a snap. The sound of the voice she had never thought to hear again made her pale. Her fingers tightened on the receiver.

"Apollo?" she whispered in disbelief. It couldn't be him. He was gone, taken by a bullet meant for her.

"Bus terminal. An hour. Waiting."

The line went dead. Suzanne stared at the phone. "It can't be. He's dead." But it was. Even if she hadn't recognized the voice, she would have felt the sudden alertness of her senses. Adrenaline was pumping

through her bloodstream. Danger, sharp and too
damn seductive, sang its siren call. But more than that
was the need to see with her own eyes that Benny still
lived. Pushing the manifest into the top drawer, she
yanked her purse from the bottom. Darin came to the
door of her office just as she got to her feet.

"Going out?"

Only training kept her tone calm, unhurried, when
every nerve screamed for the release of swift action.
"An unexpected appointment. I don't know when I'll
be back. Do me a favor and call James and tell him
I'm sorry about lunch."

"Surely you can do that your—"

Suzanne stopped his protest with a look. "If I
could, I wouldn't have asked you to do it for me." She
was already halfway through the shop. She was never
sharp with Darin or for that matter with anyone. It
was completely out of her present character.

"Are you all right?" Darin demanded worriedly,
following her.

"I'm fine." Suzanne moved through the front door
without more of an explanation. Benny needed her.
She could feel it. A bullet, she'd thought, had put an
end to their partnership. The danger they had shared,
the moments when each had depended on the other for
safety, in one case for their very lives, had forged ties
that transcended physical bonds. She regretted breaking the date with James, but she had no choice. Benny
knew she was out of the business. He would not have
contacted her unless there was a dire emergency.
Hadn't he spent three years letting her believe he was
dead? The pain resurfaced, and she silently cursed a

past filled with secrets, lies and deceptions. But she had understood that life. Hated it as much as she needed it, as much as the world needed it.

"Are you sure she didn't say anything else?" James frowned at the short message Darin had just delivered. "She didn't say where she was going?"

"No. And she was acting strangely. I've never seen her like this before. Usually she's so calm. She never raises her voice or snaps at people. She even looked different. Kind of wired."

The frown deepened to a scowl. "All right. Thanks for the message, and let me know if she checks in."

"I'm sure she'll call you—"

James cut him off. "She knows I have to be out of the office today." He was lying, but Darin couldn't know that.

James hung up, not wanting to prolong the conversation. He turned his chair so that he could stare out the window, contemplating the New Orleans skyline. He had an appointment with Cord Darcourte in an hour. He was going to build a house. Sharing his life with Suzanne had taught him that his home wasn't a home at all. Only four walls enclosing a decorator's showcase. He wanted more. He wanted a little land, privacy, large rooms, maybe a fireplace or two like Suzanne had in her house. They could lie on a rug talking, sipping wine or just being together. It was going to be his surprise if, no *when*, she agreed to move in with him.

"Where is she?"

The words were torn out of him. Something wasn't right. He could feel it, and his instincts were finely developed. One didn't claw his way to the top of the financial heap without learning the value of man's supposedly primitive responses. He didn't know why, how or what he was reacting to, but he couldn't deny he was reacting. Getting to his feet, he paced the room, hoping the phone would ring. He left for Darcourte Architects, Inc. still hoping. He talked with his old friend Cord and Cord's partner, Victoria Wynne about his need for a house. What should have been an enjoyable meeting turned into an exercise in concentration. His mind wasn't on the future. Suzanne held all his thoughts.

Suzanne entered the bus station, looking so unlike herself no one would have recognized her. Gone was the cream silk suit that she had been wearing when Benny called. In its place was a plaid shirt, faded jeans and an oversize bag slung from her shoulder. Her makeup was gone, her hair pulled back in an unbecoming style. The graceful carriage that had always attracted attention was a slouchy walk. Nothing could alter the elegant bone structure or the slender build. But neither were noticed, for Suzanne now looked nondescript and travel weary.

Where was he, she wondered, wandering with no obvious pattern. Her eyes, hidden behind dark glasses, scanned the crowd as she paused at the magazine rack. Then she saw him. He, too, wore a disguise, one she recognized and, oddly, the counterpart to her own. She sauntered closer. He smiled invitingly, a man on the make to an available woman. She smiled back, joining him.

"I'm new in town. Just get in?" Benny asked.

"Nope. Waiting for someone, but he didn't show." Their eyes met. The all clear had been established.

Benny hefted a worn duffel bag. "Can I buy you a cup of coffee?"

Suzanne shrugged. "Yeah, sure, why not."

Walking side by side, they entered the small café and chose a back booth, where anyone coming in could be easily scrutinized. Benny leaned back in his seat, to all outward appearances, relaxed.

"Retirement agrees with you, babe," he murmured, his real voice emerging in a husky drawl.

Suzanne played the game as well as he. "It has its moments. One of the worst was standing beside the grave of a friend of mine." She watched him closely. If she hadn't known him so well, she would have missed the spasm of pain that flickered across his face.

"There were reasons."

"There always are." She shrugged, smiling at the waitress who brought their coffee. Sipping slowly, she waited for him to continue.

"You aren't going to make this easy for me, are you?"

"Should I?"

"Do you think I like what happened?" He watched her, judging her reactions. He would use her because he had to. He was between a rock and a hard place, and she was the only cushion left.

"The man I thought I knew wouldn't have. You, I'm not too sure about." The hours she had spent regretting her part in the ill-fated mission were vivid memories she couldn't ignore. "I wouldn't have done that to you."

His smile held no humor. "You would have. We both know it. I trained you. You've got the nerve of a marauding tiger and the cunning of a hunter and the logic of a computer. If you had known the stakes, you would have done what I did and more, if necessary. That accusation was the woman in you talking."

"You noticed."

She should have known Benny would sense the changes in her. There was a lifetime of difference between living on the edge and leading a normal life. For both their sakes she hoped she hadn't lost her battle alertness.

"I've always noticed. I just never pushed because I knew I wasn't the right man. And you aren't the right woman. Why mess up a good partnership with a lot of hot sex."

She laughed. "I had forgotten how blunt you can be." Her anger receded; humor and acceptance returned. Three years of missing him disappeared. "You're a rat. But you have your uses."

He grinned, obviously relaxing for the first time since he had recognized her. "I wasn't sure you would come," he admitted. "I tried telling myself we had been through too much for you to let me down, but I couldn't help remembering and wondering what I would have done if the situations had been reversed."

Suzanne studied him, taking in the changes of three years. There were few. A new line here, a bit more muscle there. "I don't have to wonder. You would have come for the glorious privilege of punching me in the nose.''

He finished his coffee in one swallow. "Let's get out of here. We need to talk." He tossed two bills on the table.

Suzanne rose. "I don't think I like the sound of this."

"Believe me, I know I don't." They left the bus station. "Where's your car?"

"A block away."

"Old habits."

"A man once taught me survival skills. Besides, the walking is good for the figure."

They reached the car without attracting any unwanted attention. Suzanne knew Benny was watching his back as she was watching hers. She didn't understand what had brought him to her, but she knew it had to be big. Once an operative was out of the business, he was really out of the business. She drove north from New Orleans, not wanting to risk running into anyone she knew. The sun was bright in the sky. Under other circumstances, she would have enjoyed a drive in the country.

Benny took off his glasses and rubbed his eyes. "I hate flying. A body wasn't meant to cross so many time zones."

Suzanne glanced at him, seeing the exhaustion in his rugged face. Benjamin Forsythe, code name, Apollo, Benny only to her and his late mother. He wasn't handsome. His features taken one by one might make some describe him as ugly. His body was lanky, seeming to be all limbs. Dusty brown hair and sleepy hazel eyes were nondescript. Yet every negative was a cleverly disguised positive trait. Those eyes were sleepy only by intent. He saw more with a glance than most noticed in an hour's careful scrutiny. That loose-limbed body was tough, extremely competent in self-defense, a number of which were ancient forms such as t'ai chi. His IQ was said to be well in the higher reaches of genius, not that he would admit to it. He had a photographic memory and a gift for languages. His family had been wealthy. When the last of them died, he had inherited the whole. He had no reason she had ever discovered to work for the government. Yet he did, taking chances no one else would touch. Even now she wasn't sure what his actual department was. He had partnered her in a number of assignments, but he had also disappeared weeks at a stretch and then returned, looking older than his years demanded.

"I won't ask where you came from," she murmured, noticing something in him she had never seen before. Sex appeal. In all the years they had worked together, she had seen first the teacher and later the partner. Only today did she see the man. "No wonder you leave a trail of women behind you like confetti after a wedding."

Startled, Benny glanced at her. "What brought that on?"

She grinned. "I just realized what a sexy man you are."

Sleepy eyes lit with wicked lights. The grin that curved his lips was pure experienced male. "I tried to tell you that years ago. You wouldn't listen."

"I'm beginning to think it was the best decision I ever made," she retorted, grinning back at him. James slipped into her mind, bringing alive the passion that ebbed and flowed like a living ocean between them.

"I want to meet him," Benny said, reading her expression. "I was beginning to think this retirement stuff had gone to your head. What on earth have you been waiting for these last three years? You didn't date much, and you sure didn't go out of your way to attract any notice. What were you playing at?"

Her amusement died. "I was playing at creating a life for myself away from our world. I was tired of shadows and people who killed and were killed. I wanted a normal life, damn it."

Benny shook his head. "Boring is more like it. You should have known better. You can't force a change that drastic," he pointed out flatly.

"Well, I did it."

"No, you didn't." He hesitated then decided for shock value. "You've been seeing a guy named Southerland. You two are an item, according to my sources." He watched her stiffen. "Does he know about you?"

Suzanne clenched her jaws against the temper aching for expression. Guiding the car off the road, she parked under the shade of a tree. They were shielded from view and still able to keep watch on their back trail. Turning in her seat, she looked at him with narrowed eyes. "I didn't know you had taken up spying on your past friends."

"Low blow."

Having Benny search her out for whatever reason was one thing. Having him spy on her relationship with James, she would not tolerate. "Get to the point. You only brought up James to let me know you meant business, but you should remember I don't cave in under pressure. I'll be led, but I won't be pushed."

Benny sighed. There were parts of his job he hated. "I had to know how deeply entrenched you were in this town and with your friends. We're in trouble. Big trouble."

That got her attention. For Benny to admit a problem, it had to be really large scale. "What kind of trouble?" She wasn't ready to forget he had tried to use James, but she would listen.

"A leak. High level. A mole."

A horrible thought struck. "How long?"

His eyes held hers. Personal feelings, rights and needs disappeared at the magnitude of the threat.

"Shortly before my supposed demise. You were to be the next target."

"That's why you let me believe it was my fault you were killed." Two and two still made six in the world she had known.

"I knew you. You had always been more attached to people than I could be. I knew how I would have felt if it had been you. I banked on you bailing out."

"Knowing you, there was a backup plan if I didn't."

He nodded. "Yes, but it doesn't matter now. I've worked on this thing for three years. Being dead has some very distinct advantages. I've narrowed the leak down to two people—our boss and his superior. The problem is that one knows I'm among the living and the other doesn't."

"What do you want me to do?"

"I have a plan."

"You always do."

He ignored the sarcasm. It felt good to be in harness with her again. Of all the women he knew, she was the only one he fully trusted. "You'll help me." He could have made his statement a question if for no other reason than friendship. But he didn't play games and neither did she.

"You covered your bets. Don't pretend to be surprised. You would have used James against me. You would have destroyed my life here to get my cooperation."

"I would have hated doing it."

"Expendable weapons, beasts of burdens. That's us." The bitterness surprised them both.

"You've changed."

"Did you think I wouldn't?"

He frowned. "Have you lost the edge?"

Suzanne shifted restlessly. "Three years is a long time, and I did my best to kill the past." To lie would be to put them both at risk.

"Damn! I counted on you. There isn't anyone else. I can't tell the enemies from the friends anymore." He stared out the window.

Suzanne touched his arm, drawing his attention. "Count me in. I won't bail out. You have my word."

"I wish I had the time to find a better way. I knew you were a long shot. This guy has been eating our people for breakfast. I don't want to see you as the next entrée."

"Then make sure you cover my tail," she returned quickly. "Tell me what you want."

"A trap. Bait he can't refuse. I want his hide."

"You have the bait?"

"Damn straight. The complete list of the agent network in the Southern hemisphere. You're going to be the courier. Sensitive issue. The leak is no longer under wraps. Your reputation makes calling in retirement believable."

"Why doesn't our man just wait for the thing to cross his desk?"

"I made sure each knew he was being watched."

"Nasty. How did they take it?"

"Don't ask stupid questions."

She smiled faintly. Benny had a way of making a point without raising his voice or using one ounce of force more than the job needed to get done. "So when is the setup?"

"Two days. Had to be sure you'd cooperate."

She glared at him. "If I were you, I wouldn't bring that up again. I don't like being spied on, and I certainly don't like blackmail, even from you."

Benny watched her carefully. "Is he important to you?"

"Have you ever known me to be this close with anyone."

"You're evading the question."

"You don't have any right to ask it."

He paused. "So, you've drawn the battle lines. I guess I have to respect your stand or risk losing you.

Odd, I'd thought you were past trusting anyone that deeply. Even with me, you always held back. What will you tell him?''

''About what?'' She pretended ignorance, for she didn't know what to tell James. There was no way, given the closeness of their relationship, that he wouldn't notice the difference in her.

''You can't live a lie.''

''I have been for three years.''

His eyes narrowed, his expression sharpening. ''Is that what you tell yourself? How long do you think you can continue with that kind of thinking? How can you offer yourself to a man? Lying isn't in your nature. Not when it involves people you care about.''

''Don't you think I know that? What choice did I have? Oh, by the way, I used to work for the government, ferrying around sensitive documents, risking my life, risking the lives of friends and co-workers. Even got one of them killed.'' Tears stung her eyes. She wiped them away. ''You asked me about edges. I cry these days. Not much, but enough to know I haven't forgotten how to feel, in spite of the fact I lead an ordinary life. Boring, you called it. Safe, I call it. You spied on us. You know what James is. Do you think he would want me near him if he knew what I had been?''

''What makes you think he wouldn't? If he cared about you, your past wouldn't matter. And what's so terrible back there anyway? You worked for your government. Some would call that noble.''

''Just forget it.'' Suzanne started the car. ''I assume you'll let me know when and where.''

"What I saw and heard of your man, I liked. I would've liked meeting him."

Suzanne walked out of the elevator, glancing at her watch. She was late. James should already be home. She had her story ready, even to the extent of covering her tracks by visiting a client with the collection of Victorian fly catchers one of her other clients, a European, was interested in purchasing. That was why she was an hour late now. Sighing, hating the lie she knew she would tell in the next few minutes, she entered the apartment.

James came out of the kitchen, a frown on his face. "That must have been some client," he murmured, coming toward her. He pulled her close and kissed her deeply. "I hope it was worth it, because I'm starving."

Suzanne didn't have time to cool her response. James received the full brunt of the passion she usually paced to match his. Her tongue dueled with his, demanding his desire as ardently as he had ever commanded hers.

James raised his head, breathing heavily. The frown was gone. In its place was a need that showed in the glitter of his eyes and the hard thrust of his hips against hers. "I don't know what brought this on, but I like it," he muttered, dipping his head for another sample. "Let's forget dinner completely," he suggested roughly, a moment later. Sweeping her into his arms, he headed for the bedroom.

Suzanne clung to him, caught in the mesh of their mutual need. Now that she had betrayed herself, she found she wasn't sorry. She wanted to know the full extent of their passion. She wanted to go up in flames. She wanted him to burn so that he would never want another woman but her. The ties she had avoided suddenly seemed the most important thing in the world. The morning might bring regrets, but this night was for the real woman, not the illusion she had created.

Eight

The sun pouring in the windows woke Suzanne early. She lay cradled in James's arms, watching the flickering shadows paint pictures on his bare torso. Pleasurable aches in various muscles reminded her of the passion they had shared through the night. James had been pleased though puzzled at her sudden change from the willing partner she had been to a woman who knew her own power and offered her man a taste of her desire. She, too, was puzzled. It was as though the lifting of the guilt of her part in Benny's supposed death had freed her somehow. The fear of touching and being touched by her deepest feelings was easing with every hour. The untruths of the life she had built for herself were more blatant, more impossible to tolerate.

And James. She had met him in the illusion. He had never lied to her. She knew he wanted the woman she had pretended to be. Would he still want her now? Her eyes darkened at the thought. Her hands clenched in an effort not to touch, not to awaken him. She wanted to tell him about her past. Benny was right. She had been a fool to lie. But now more than ever, she had to remain silent. Not for the illusion, not for the fear of her own emotions, but for the man she had come to love.

Love. She loved James. She hadn't wanted to. She hadn't allowed herself to wonder why she had agreed to consider moving in with him. To think too deeply was to find the truth. She had been living an illusion, but there was nothing illusionary about her feelings for James. She loved him with all the facets of her nature. He had taught her passion in a way no man had. He had given her security and caring, laughter and understanding. She had repaid him in lies.

And now, because of her, he stood in danger. By agreeing to help Benny, she was reentering the world of shadows, of rules that had little to do with fairness and where a life was sometimes less important than names on a list. The man she and Benny hunted would protect himself at all costs. If Benny had found her and discovered James's significance in her life, then their adversary could, too.

"Frowning this early?" James rolled on his side, his fingers tracing the lines between her brows. "I thought I made you happy."

She dredged up a smile. "You did." Sliding closer, she fitted her body to his. His warmth surrounded her, his scent rich and seductive. Desire spiraled within. One more time. She would taste their passion one more time.

"I was lonely. That's why I was frowning."

His lips trailed kisses along her jawline, pausing at the hollow in her throat. "You should have awakened me. I was lonely, too."

She arched as his breath warmed her skin. Her hands threaded through his hair. "We're going to be late."

"I don't care. I'm busy loving my woman."

"Get a move on, honey. We really are going to be late." James collected her handbag as Suzanne stepped into her shoes.

"It's not my fault you decided we should share a shower," she pointed out.

He shrugged. "I hate scrubbing my own back. Besides, you do a better job."

She took her purse and brushed a kiss against his lips as she evaded his arms. "As I recall, you were the one doing the washing."

"A mere technicality."

The banter continued during the elevator ride down to the parking garage. Their cars sat side by side. James walked with her to hers. "Did you leave your window down last night?" He frowned at the sleek little BMW, looking for signs of tampering. "That's not like you."

"I was in a hurry to get home." Suzanne pushed the memory of the day before away. She didn't want anything to spoil this morning.

James stared at the splash of mud covering the left rear tire and part of the bumper. The small twig from a pine tree stuck in the trim was even more of a surprise. He had taken Suzanne's car to the car wash on Sunday, two days ago. It had been spotlessly clean when she had left for work yesterday. Puzzled, he turned to her. Her eyes were clear, her lips smiling. She couldn't look at him like that and be hiding something. Yet there was no reasonable explanation for the mud. New Orleans hadn't had rain in the city since a week ago Saturday. In fact, most of the south was in the midst of a drought, which was why he was aware that the only rainfall had been in the parish north of them—a rural area, an area thick with pine trees.

Then he remembered. Darin lived north of New Orleans. He could have borrowed Suzanne's car. He had before. Feeling guilty for his vague suspicions, he pulled her into his arms.

"I just discovered I'm a jealous man," he muttered, his mouth against her hair.

Suzanne touched his face, smiling without understanding. "About what?"

"That." He pointed to the mud. "You told me where you were yesterday. I saw that, and just for a moment I wondered if you had lied to me. Sorry, honey."

Suzanne fought every instinct to stiffen in his arms. It had never been more difficult to play her role. "What convinced you I hadn't lied?"

"I know you. And before I could forget how honest you are in your dealings, I remembered that Darin lives north of the city, which is the only place where anyone could have gotten into a mud puddle in this drought. I figured you loaned him your car again."

"I never realized what an observant man you are," she murmured, just managing to conceal her shock at his accurate pinpointing of her movements despite his erroneous assumption of who was doing the moving.

"We're even then. I never realized the fire that existed in you. I like knowing we burn together." He kissed her once, hard and deep, then urged her into the car. "Now go to work, woman, and remember today is my lunch, no one else's."

Suzanne drove away, fighting the tears in her eyes. She was well and truly caught in a trap. And James had just shown her how to free him from the danger she was entering. Another lie would be born, another illusion to live, to hate. The first thing she did when she reached her office was to dial the number Benny had given her in case of emergencies. He answered on the second ring.

"I need you."

"Problems? Our man?" His voice was deceptively soft and slow.

Suzanne turned her head to stare out the window. "Yes and no, in that order. An hour. You know where." She hung up the phone, her eyes glued to the scene outside. Using every ounce of willpower she possessed, she fought the tears threatening her composure. If Benny saw them, he would understand too much. If she gave in to them, she would be too weak to go through with her plan. Too much was at stake: lives, security, her own integrity. Benny's life. If he had breached one of their most ironclad rules by coming to her, then he had no other choice, no one but her to help.

"Suzanne?" Darin stared at her rigid back.

Taking a deep breath, she swung around. "Do you need me?"

He shook his head. "Are you all right?"

She forced a smile. "Fine. Just thinking. I have to go out for a bit. Watch the store for me."

Nodding, he continued to study her. "I make a good listener if I put my mind to it."

Suzanne picked up her handbag to avoid looking at him. One of the disadvantages of her new life was the friends she had made. In the past there had been few close relationships that allowed for implied questions like Darin's. "Some business only. A bit of a nuisance but no real problem." She touched his arm as she passed. "It will be over in a few days anyway. No sweat." The slang slipped out. She noted his frown and damned her unguarded words. Three years and she hadn't made a mistake, hadn't once gotten her identities mixed. In the space of two days she had botched it twice. Not a good record. Squaring her shoulders, she walked out of the shop. Slips cost lives.

The drive to the park across town took a half hour. Suzanne used the time to pull herself back into the past, to reactivate the senses she had allowed to atrophy.

Benny was waiting under the trees where he had a good view of the open area around him. She strolled across the green, her eyes alert for anyone who might be taking undue interest in their meeting. She slid an arm through his and leaned her head against his shoulder. She felt him stiffen slightly.

"Company?" he asked as he bent his head to brush her lips with a kiss that held nothing but an appearance of affection.

"Cautious. You know me." She returned the greeting, feeling a traitor to James even though there wasn't an ounce of physical awareness in the gesture.

"Why?"

She didn't need the question clarified. "James means a lot to me. I don't want him involved. You found me and knew about him. Others can, too. I want him publicly out."

She looked into his eyes, putting on her most loving expression. The perception in the hazel gaze probed too deeply, but she didn't turn away. "James is too perceptive for me to use some flimsy excuse or setup. I need something that will make him force a break between us. The only avenue open is his jealousy. I got the idea this morning when he saw the mud on the tires and a few pieces of pine branch caught in the bumper and figured out where I was yesterday. For a minute he was really worked up. If I can just use that, channel it, he'll walk away from me long enough for us to get this done."

Benny gave a low whistle of admiration. "You're taking a big chance with a setup like that. If he means anything to you, what will you do if you can't make it right with him afterward?" He watched her carefully, adding, "That was sloppy work, Athena, getting caught in the first place. You used to be sharper than that."

Her face was blank and as smooth as marble as she stared back at him. "I've gone soft. You're really scraping the bottom of the barrel with me on this one. Or maybe I was already setting this thing in motion with James."

Only an insensitive fool would have accepted the last as truth. Despite her best intentions, he could see the pain in her eyes for what she would do to James. He honored them both by not making more of an issue of her words.

"I don't think so, and I'm not scraping the bottom of any barrel." He stopped and pulled her against him. His grasp looked loverlike; however, it was anything but. His hands moved over her arms, down her back, outlining sleek muscles toned by constant exercise and t'ai chi. "You're in better shape now than three years ago. I should know. And that mind of yours might be a little out of tune, but I'd put it against some of the best in the business and still give odds." He leaned forward and kissed her, this time meaning it as one friend to another, one partner who had shared danger with another.

"So you found your man?" He tucked her hand in his and continued walking. "I don't think this plan of yours is very bright. Your James isn't one to put up with another guy in his territory. If he cares for you at all, he'll make your life miserable. And on top of that I don't think you're going to be able to convince him that there is nothing between us when you do tell him the truth. We have a lot of history. It shows. Besides, in certain circles we have played the lovers."

"I know. Don't you think that if I had time I wouldn't come up with a better way?" She glared at him.

He flicked her chin. "Careful! The trees could have eyes."

"I hate this."

His glance sharpened at the comment. Drawing her into the shadows of the trees, he caged her against a tree trunk. "You want out? Don't lie to me because you think I need you. It won't do either of us any good if you don't have your brains in line for this. You know what's at stake. I'd rather go alone than worry about you caving in."

"I'm not backing out. I said I'd help and I will. But the edge is gone. I can feel it." Wrapping her hands around his wrists, she tightened her fingers. "There was a time when I rode the crest of danger, knowing I could fall and laughing at the risk. The higher the wave, the greater the stake, the better. Then I thought you died. The bottom fell out of the world. The wave crashed and slammed me into the ocean bottom. I tasted fear. Not of dying. But of losing myself. I ran. You found me." She searched his face, willing him to understand. "But before you came back, there was James. He made me feel again. A week or a month from now, I might have found my balance. Love and fear are two powerful emotions I don't know very well. I'm not sure I can cope."

"You know Athena is the goddess of wisdom in Greek mythology. I always thought someone had screwed up when they named you. Now I'm not so sure."

"Why? Because I'm admitting I'm an emotional basket case?"

"No. Because you're wise enough to learn from your past and brave enough to face fear and push through. I wish I could tell you I don't need you. I wish I could think of a better way of protecting your man. I can't. But I'll tell you this. When we get out of this with our skins intact, I promise you I'll do everything I can to make sure you don't lose." His hands cupped her face. "Deal?"

The tears pooled in her eyes. She smiled anyway. "I hate crying women."

"On you, even they look good." His thumbs caught the two drops that escaped and brushed them away. "If he could see us now, you wouldn't need any more window dressing."

"I know." She sighed. "He's coming to pick me up for lunch. I want you to follow me back to the shop, and we'll let him walk in on us. Nothing too blatant or he'll smell a setup even if he doesn't understand why. I wish I could get rid of Darin for a few hours, but we might need him to corroborate the breakup."

"Then what?"

"Dinner tonight, I guess."

"You want me to stay over at your apartment, too?"

Suzanne hesitated. Her mind had shied away from the horrible conclusion.

"If I were him, I wouldn't be put off by a kiss or two."

Suzanne closed her eyes for a moment, gathering strength. "The couch isn't too bad as a bunk." The words left an acid taste in her mouth.

"You could tell him some of the truth. Or tell him you have to go out of town for a few days."

She opened her eyes, reading the compassion in his. "It would serve for getting me away from him, maybe. But it wouldn't lessen his danger if our quarry wants to use him for leverage."

"Damned if you do and damned if you don't." Exhaling deeply, he dropped his arms. "Let's get this show on the road. I'm beginning to think you had the right idea to retire, regardless of the reasons. Sometimes I hate these lies and hurting people to protect them. And more than any of that, I hate not having friends and someone to come back to."

Suzanne stared at him, as shocked by his words as he must have been by hers earlier. "That doesn't sound like you."

He smiled grimly. "I've been in this business a hell of a lot longer than you. I've piled up a load of regrets and one of the worst was letting you think I died and that you were partially responsible. I knew what it would do to you and I did it anyway." He stared straight ahead, his jaw clenched. "Did I tell you I was sorry?"

"No. And I wouldn't have listened if you had. You did what you had to do, just like I'm going to now. James may never believe me, even if I can get him to listen to my explanation when this is over. We knew the risks then and now. We can't play the game any other way."

"You tried."

"I failed."

"You found your man."

"He wants what he thinks I am, not what I really am. I played the role so well that he doesn't see the woman beneath the mask. And if he did, I don't think he'd want her."

"My God!" Benny breathed as they reached her car. "The man's a fool."

"No." She shook her head. "Far from it. He's honest and fair. Far more than I am." She opened the car door and got in. "Ready?"

"Do we have a choice?" He turned away to cross the street to the rental car he had leased under a fictitious name.

"Back so soon?" Darin glanced up from the counter he was rearranging.

"The meeting didn't take as long as I expected. I'll be in my office if you need me."

Suzanne sat down in the chair and closed her eyes. Benny would give her a few minutes before he made his entrance. He would stop to speak to Darin, make the appropriate remarks to establish himself as a past lover, then he would join her. Darin would be shocked. She heard the door to the office open. His footsteps were soft. The hands that lifted her from the chair gentle. Her eyes opened, catching a glimpse of Darin's face just before Benny took her in his arms.

"You are one tough woman to find, love." His lips took hers, stealing the supposed surprised protest from her lips.

Suzanne faked her response to the very ardent-looking kiss. Benny broke his hold the moment the door closed behind Darin. Suzanne sank into the chair and stared up at him.

"Act one over."

Benny perched on the edge of the desk. "That should give your young friend just enough embarrassment to make him act very guilty when James comes in. The closed door is a nice touch." He glanced at the clock. "Is he usually late or early?"

"Early."

"It figures." He studied her. "You're going to have to work at looking a tad radiant. Remember, I'm your long-lost lover. Pretend I'm him if it helps."

"Nothing's going to help this." She rested her head in her hands. "You'd better invite yourself along to lunch."

He frowned at her bent head. "You want to go that far?"

"As you said, you wouldn't give up if you were James. I have a feeling he's every bit as stubborn as you. And I sure haven't been giving the slightest impression of holding back."

"Just make sure we don't end up at a restaurant that serves arsenic."

A soft knock at the door interrupted them.

"Show time," Benny muttered, quickly running his fingers through his hair so that it was ruffled as though from a woman's passionate hands. A flick of his wrist sent pins cascading from Suzanne's hair as the red-gold mass tumbled to her shoulders. Another flick and two buttons on her blouse were loosened.

"This isn't a striptease," Suzanne hissed, doing up one. "Come in," she called before he could do any more damage. She knew the exact moment that James took in the scene. She felt his anger emanate in waves across the room, slamming into her as she turned her head to look at him.

She was wrong. It wasn't anger. It was pure fury. A man's rage flashed in his eyes. His hands clenched at his sides. His whole body was taut as if drawn on a rack. Suzanne swallowed the sickness in her heart at his searing glare. She felt rather than saw Benny turn.

"Hello. Who's this?" He rose, playing his role with the flair that had made him one of the best in the business. He held out his hand, introducing himself.

James ignored the gesture and the man who made it. All he could see was Suzanne. The look in her eyes made him ill. The knowledge that another man had held her, kissed her, run his hands through her hair, maybe burned in the same fire that had consumed him just hours before lit a rage in him like none he had ever known.

"Get out!" He glanced once at the man called Benny. Hate was a red tide.

Benny folded his arms, regretting what was coming, knowing they were in too far to pull back. For a moment he felt admiration for the man before him. His control was phenomenal. When this was over, he would do his best to see that Suzanne had another chance with her lover.

"I was invited. Were you?" Benny cocked a brow, putting match to the tinder of masculine temper. He would be lucky if he didn't get a broken jaw out of this piece of business.

James took a step forward. Benny tensed. Suzanne sprang from her chair and threw herself between them.

"Stop it. Both of you. I'm not a bone to be fought over."

James glared at her. "Did you invite him here?"

"Yes."

He backed up a step, not completely believing it until then. Suddenly another thought struck. "Did you loan Darin your car yesterday?"

Suzanne braced herself against what was coming. "No."

"You were with him."

"She was." Benny put his arm around her shoulders, knowing Suzanne was close to the end of her rope. They had to finish, but it didn't have to be as bad as this. "She thought I was dead until yesterday. Three years ago there was an accident. She was there." He glanced down at her, reading her surprise at the truth. "I came because I needed her. No one else would do. It really wasn't her fault. If you blame anyone, blame me."

James stared at him, then at Suzanne as she leaned against him. The familiarity of their pose told of a deep relationship. Angry as he was, he hadn't missed the looks they exchanged. Secrets were in their eyes. Suzanne was pale, but he couldn't tell if it was from shock or distress.

"I want to talk to you alone. I think you owe me that," he said, forcing the words out.

Benny stepped in before Suzanne could answer. "I think not. Let her be for a few days. My coming like this has knocked her off balance. Why don't we both back off and give her a chance to pull herself together?"

Suzanne sent him a grateful look. Benny was giving her breathing space. She wouldn't have to hurt James so very much this way.

"Is that what you want, Suzanne?"

She nodded without looking at him. If she did, she wouldn't be able to finish.

James jammed his hands into his pockets. The urge to slug something or someone was too strong. "And where will you be?"

Benny grinned. The belligerence was understandable and frankly something he shared. Life was no picnic. Damn, if he didn't like this guy. "In my lonely bed, if you must know. I don't cheat, and I don't take unfair advantage."

James couldn't decide what he was feeling. Damn this Benny character. There was nothing remotely funny about this situation, but he found it was almost impossible not to see something odd in those hazel eyes watching him so closely. Suzanne was acting completely out of character. She wasn't the kind of woman to lie or to let others make plans for her. Uneasy without understanding why, James studied them carefully. Little things were often more important than large ones, a business maxim he had found invariably correct over the years.

"Why don't you go home, love, and let Darin take care of the store for the rest of the day?" Benny suggested. Suzanne hadn't mistaken the measure of James. The man was sharp. Already he was beginning to question their little scenario.

Suzanne roused herself enough to nod. She wanted out, away from both men. But more than anything, she wanted a bath and the oblivion of sleep. The need to cleanse away the lies and escape the future was strong and, for this moment, safe to give in to. Tomorrow would come soon enough, and then she would be strong.

Nine

Suzanne climbed the stairs, wishing she hadn't left James and Benny alone in her office. Yet Benny had seen that she had had no other choice. Frowning, she started to put the key into the door when she realized it was ajar. Instantly her senses went to full alert. Wrapping the strap of her handbag around her hand, she created a weapon. Easing the door open, she scanned the room.

Chaos. Drawers pulled out. Chairs overturned. A sound from her bedroom. She tensed. The intruder was still there. She padded forward, her face cool and expressionless although her eyes burned with anger. She slipped off her heels and edged closer. She made no sound as she entered the dim bedroom. The man was bent over her dresser, rooting in the bottom drawer. Her gaze checked for weapons. None. A soundless sigh of relief escaped. Two steps carried her to his back. He whirled, instinct working when no sound had betrayed her.

"Damn!" He swore, coming erect.

Suzanne bent and swung, connecting with a debilitating t'ai chi move. The man staggered sideways, sweeping a lamp into her path. Wasting no time in defending himself, he fled with her hot on his heels. Hampered by the tight skirt, Suzanne lost him on the steps. Angry at not capturing him and furious that her home had been invaded, she stalked into the apartment, slamming and bolting the door.

Benny would not be pleased. She glared at the mess, deciding she might as well pick up while she waited for Benny to return to his hotel room. The last thing she wanted to do was alert James by calling Benny at the shop, assuming both men were still there, of course. The thought deepened her frown. She didn't want to remember the scene in her office. She didn't want to remember the look on James's face when he thought she and Benny were past lovers. She hurt. Her fingers touched her lips. His taste was more than a memory. It was pain. Supposing she couldn't get him back when she and Benny were done. And if she could? Could she live the lie of the illusion he wanted? Her life was in a worse state than her apartment, she thought cynically, putting the last drawer in place. Work had eased her temper, but nothing could ease her mind.

She dialed Benny.

"What's wrong?" he asked sharply, on hearing her voice.

"I had a visitor."

"Damn! Are you all right?"

"Fine. And my apartment survived, too." She sank into the chair beside the phone and rubbed her temple. A headache was building. Tension. Frustration.

"I'll be right over."

"That's not necessary," she protested, not wanting company.

He ignored her refusal. "There's more. Check that place for bugs before I get there."

She glared at the phone that buzzed the dial tone. She had forgotten how much she disliked orders, especially terse, uninformative ones. But dislike didn't keep her from obeying. The place was clean of listening devices, although it might not have been if she had come home at the regular time. The doorbell rang. She went to let Benny in.

"There's a rip in your skirt," he murmured, giving her a thorough look over.

Suzanne shrugged. "What did you expect? I found the creep going through my lingerie drawer. I chased him halfway down the stairs in this get-up. You try it and see if you don't end up with a rip or two. And this outfit was brand-new."

"Gorgeous thing it is, too," he murmured before taking a seat. His amusement died as she sat down across from him. "We've got problems. Rick called. It seems Danfield is our man. This time he's sure."

Suzanne's eyes widened at the blunt pronouncement. Danfield was their immediate supervisor and the man with the names of all field personnel in his mind. A career serviceman with top security clearance, he was dangerous, smart and too well-informed to be allowed to run free. He had to be caught or stopped. "They got him?"

Benny's expression was fierce, a mixture of anger and frustration. "Not bloody likely. He blew town. Took a top-secret file, one that any government in the world would pay with their lifeblood to get."

"So much for your plan to flush him out."

"Yeah. But that's not the worst of it. Rick trailed him as far as a Concorde to England. Lost him at Heathrow."

"What now? Do you have a line on where he might be heading, or is it time to play hunt for the needle in the haystack?"

"A little bit of both. But you don't need to worry. I'm going after him alone."

"Alone? To borrow your expression, not bloody likely. I'm not bailing out on this. I'm in too deep and I want this guy as bad as you. Friends of mine are at risk, yourself included. For that matter, I'm also on the hot seat and we both know it."

"Trying to sell me on selfish motivations, are you? It won't wash. I know you too well. But you're forgetting we won't have any backup. Rick still isn't sure who was in on this and who wasn't. Other than him—and he's tied up running the department until they can get a replacement for Danfield—it will be just you and me, kid."

Suzanne stared him straight in the eyes, refusing the freedom he offered. "I'm still going with you. We've been in worse fixes and made it with each other's help. You need me, so don't try pretending you don't."

"No." He glared at her. The price she'd paid to help him was already too high. "I don't need you."

She almost smiled at the temper in his voice. "You're lying and we both know it."

Benny decided to try a different tack. "Your business?"

"Darin."

He'd hurt her to stop her. "James?"

The pain came and went in her eyes, banished by control so deeply ingrained that she didn't notice it. "Later."

"There might not be one. They know you in Europe. Your name heads the top of a lot of lists."

"Give me a better plan."

Neither backed down. Both knew the score.

"When do we leave?"

One last attempt. "You know there is no time limit on how long. Weeks. Months, maybe."

"When, Apollo?"

"I hate it when you use my code name. That's when you're the most stubborn. I never have won with you in that mood." He shrugged and got to his feet. "An hour. I'll help you pack."

"No, you will pack. I have a note to write."

He glanced at her sharply. "James?"

She nodded once before going to the desk and pulling out a piece of paper. "There's a black case in the back of the closet. Use it."

James stared at the envelope in his hand. Suzanne. He recognized her writing. Odd. He had waited all day for her call, and now he was hesitating at opening a

simple letter. Angered, he ripped the envelope so that
the single sheet fell out. He swore steadily, vehe-
mently as he read the three lines.

"I have gone away for a while to think. I don't
know when or if I'll return. Take care of yourself."

His hand crushed the stationery, and he threw it
across the room. "I won't let you do this," he raged.
"A note is not enough, woman." He reached for his
jacket and slammed out of the apartment. His mind
wasn't on his driving as he crossed town to her place.
The building was dark. He didn't care. She couldn't be
gone yet. Her car was still in the driveway. He took the
stairs two at a time. Loud knocking on her door pro-
duced nothing. A two-hour wait on the stairs pro-
duced her friend's arrival and the same explanation
that Suzanne had written him. She was going away.

"Was she alone?" he demanded suddenly. He
didn't want to think she had lied.

Pat shook her head, looking uncomfortable. "No.
There was a man with her."

"Rangy, hazel eyes, moves easy, like he has no
bones in his body?" he asked grimly.

"Yes." Pat glanced at her door. "Look, it's late. I
have to work tomorrow." She edged by him, clearly
wanting to escape.

James turned away. He knew more than he wanted
to know. Suzanne had lied. She and Benny were gone
together. Jamming his clenched fists into his pockets,
he walked down the stairs to his car. He drove until he
was too tired to move. Dawn was breaking over the
city when he pulled into the underground garage. He
had a full day at the office. He had needed a good

night's sleep, not a marathon of driving around the city.

He had thought himself past being fooled by a woman. Suzanne had proved him wrong. Suddenly the house he had just commissioned Cord Darcourte to build for him in the country seemed so stupid. He had wanted Suzanne to share it with him. It would have been a surprise. Only he had gotten the surprise. Another man. A man whom, in different circumstances, he might have liked.

"You look like the devil, my friend." Cord Darcourte studied James. "In fact, now that I think about it, you have looked bad for a couple of weeks now. Want to talk about it?"

James stared at the drink in his hand. He could have told Cord to the day exactly how long it had been. There wasn't a moment when he didn't think of her. There wasn't a night he didn't reach out to hold her silken body. There wasn't a redhead in the whole city who hadn't caught his eye, for an instant making him wonder if Suzanne had returned.

"Did you invite me to your place just to poke about in my mind?"

He lifted his glass and took a swallow. He wouldn't have accepted Cord's invitation if staying at home hadn't become so painful of late. Her memory lived in his apartment, taunting him with the passionate past when she had given her body and filled his mind with her lies. He wanted to hate her for the dishonesty and the man. He couldn't for either. It would have been easier if he could.

"Nope. It's called misery loves company." Cord drained his own glass before getting up. "Want a refill?"

James shook his head. "It won't help."

Cord nodded. "I suppose not." He flung himself back into the chair and closed his eyes. "Women are made to drive us crazy. You play the game. You wait. You go slow. And always you watch. I'm getting older. I want more than I used to."

James surfaced from his own pain enough to know Cord was hurting, too. "You want to talk about it?"

Cord shook his head, the gesture weary, his expression resigned. "Won't help. Tell me why you quit pushing on with the house, instead."

James shrugged. "The need for it isn't there anymore."

"Suzanne."

James jerked erect. "You know?"

"Half the city knows. You didn't make your liaison a secret. Are you the reason she left?"

James laughed grimly. "No. I wish I were."

Cord was neither stupid nor insensitive. "Then you're better off without her. A woman shouldn't play one man off against another. They hold most of the aces anyway."

"The voice of experience."

Cord grinned recklessly. "My share only."

"I know better despite your celibate ways of late."

"Maybe we both need to look around and find us a lady each. No sense in being miserable when it doesn't change anything."

"Don't want another woman."

"Yeah, well neither do I, but I also don't relish nights like this one, either."

James frowned. "Got a point." He glanced down at the empty glass he held. "How many of these things have I had?"

"One."

"Feels like three."

"One drink and exhaustion will do that to you." Cord pushed to his feet. "I know. I've worked too long just to sleep the way you're doing. Recently in fact. You can use the guest room tonight, if you like. I'm going to bed."

James awoke the next morning with a massive headache—not a hangover—and a resolution. Cord was right. He might as well accept the fact that Suzanne wanted no part of his life. She had made her choice. The problem was that he didn't know any women he wanted except Suzanne, but it was time he found one, someone who knew the score, someone who wouldn't expect more than he had to give. But first he had to deal with his house. He hadn't been fair to Cord or himself. Just because Suzanne didn't want him didn't mean he had to roll over and die. He would build his house.

The thought brought him out of bed with something more than a gray outlook. He had an appointment at Darcourte this morning. Instead of canceling his order, he would ask Cord to push ahead. Feeling better than he had in weeks, he showered and put on his rumpled clothes. Cord was already up and gone.

James changed at his apartment and then headed for Darcourte Architects, Inc.

Cord wasn't in, but Victoria was. Their meeting was short due to his own commitments, although plans were made to meet for dinner to clear up the details still remaining. Satisfied with the first step on his road to recovering from Suzanne, James went to his office and put in a full day.

The night was dark, moonless. The smell of garbage and unwashed bodies was strong in the air in this poor section of town. Two shadows moved down the narrow alley. The larger stopped; the smaller melted into the alcove of the doorway beside him.

"Damn!" Benny swore softly.

Suzanne cocked her head, listening. The slight sounds of more breathing than hers and Benny's was unnaturally loud in the silence. "Company?" she whispered against his ear. His nod was no less than she expected. "Betrayed?"

Another nod.

The anger was swift and almost more than she could control. She had been too long out of the field. Emotions could not exist here if she wanted to survive. James. His image came to her, distracting her further. She cursed silently and slammed the mental door on pain and the specter of her future. Here and now was all she could allow to matter.

Benny touched her arm, maybe sensing her preoccupation. He signaled with a restrained movement for her to stay back while he made the contact. If he was ambushed, she might be his only hope for surviving with his skin intact. Once, such a maneuver would have been a matter of course. Now Suzanne damned the necessity even as she obeyed his command. The minutes ticked by too slowly for comfort. Suzanne stayed alert and tense as Benny spoke quietly with the man who, for a ridiculously small sum of money, was willing to spill his brains on the whereabouts of their quarry.

"Well?" Suzanne demanded when Benny joined her.

"He says Danfield's gone. That he's never been here at all. It was all a very elaborate smoke screen."

Suzanne followed him out of the alley, silently cursing Danfield for all he was worth. Benny wasn't nearly as restrained. She smiled a little at some of his more colorful and inventive comments.

"That won't help."

"Wanna bet? This has been one long farce from beginning to end. And the topper is the biggest joke of all. The creep was right on our doorstep all along."

Suzanne stared at him as he got into the car they had rented on arriving in Madrid. "What do you mean?"

"I mean Danfield has an estate right outside of New Orleans. How's that for a coincidence?"

Suzanne leaned back, closing her eyes in defeat. "Then all these weeks were for nothing. If I ever wanted a reason for why I got out of the business, I have it now." With the best will in the world she couldn't keep the bitterness out of her voice.

Benny shot her a sharp look, knowing immediately her mind was no longer on the job. "Stop thinking about James. I told you that I would help you convince him of how important this is. Why the devil don't you have a little faith in him, yourself and me? You can't keep on like this or you won't be any good to any of us. You don't sleep well. You don't eat much. And you jump at every shadow. That's not like you. Where's your perspective? Your common sense? I like the man. He's no fool. He may be angry and hurt, but he isn't beyond reach."

"You don't know James like I do," she argued, opening her eyes to glare at him. "And you also don't have any experience in what I'm feeling. So don't make judgments. There isn't any control anymore. I hate that, but I can't stop it. Do you have an idea how that makes me feel?"

"I'd think, damn lucky. You found a man worth having. So hang in there, woman. Besides, this time tomorrow we'll be back in the good ole U.S. of A. We'll get Danfield and you can get back to work on James."

"Well, did you get in touch with James?" Benny asked the moment Suzanne opened the door to her apartment.

"I didn't try," Suzanne admitted wearily. They had been traveling to get back to New Orleans for the better part of the past twenty-four hours. She was exhausted. Thinking was a major effort. "There isn't any point until we get Danfield."

Benny frowned at the defeat in her voice. "There is if you run into James," he countered sharply.

"He won't bother us. You forget what a good actor you are. He'll think just what you intended him to think. His pride will keep him from demanding an explanation.'' She picked up her jacket and slipped it on over the midnight-blue dress. "Now if we are going to eat, let's do it. I need an early night." She headed for the door without waiting to see if he would follow.

The drive to the restaurant was accomplished in silence. Suzanne was aware of the looks Benny kept giving her, but she pretended not to notice. She didn't want to talk about the mess her life was in at the moment. She didn't want to talk about anything. She wouldn't even have been going out if Benny hadn't bullied her into it. At least the restaurant Benny had chosen wasn't one that James had taken her to—a small blessing, but one for which she was grateful. With luck she would finish helping Benny without running into James.

But her luck was out of town. The first person she and Benny saw on entering the restaurant was James, in the company of the most exquisitely beautiful black-haired woman Suzanne had ever seen. The way James was bent protectively over her, told a deeper story than Suzanne wanted to know. She felt her face pale. Benny took her arm, supporting her in a way that had never been necessary.

"Are you all right?" he demanded in a rough whisper.

"Take a guess," she invited bitterly, pulling every ounce of reserve to the fore. She couldn't bear it if James could see how finding him with another woman made her feel. She had to hide the sickness clawing at her stomach, the pain clenching her heart, until it was a Herculean effort to breathe.

Suzanne knew the moment James realized she was there. She saw his eyes travel to Benny. She read the conclusion and the disdain in his expression before he tenderly escorted his date from Suzanne's presence.

Benny swore once.

"You're doing too much of that lately," she murmured, striving to pull herself together.

"I've had good reason," he muttered, guiding her to their table.

"Don't look so worried. I'll survive."

Benny glanced back at the door through which James had passed. "I thought I liked that guy. I've changed my mind. Right now I could cheerfully take his head off at his shoulders."

"Not for me, my friend." Suzanne felt the pain and bitterness slide into the dark corners of her mind, releasing her momentarily from what could not be changed. The die was cast. "I fight my own battles."

The massive headache James woke up with the next morning was no joke. He felt as if he had been run over by a semi. It took a moment for him to realize where he was. Victoria's guest room. They had come back to Victoria's apartment. He hadn't wanted to be alone and oddly, it seemed, neither had Victoria. So the evening had spun on with talk of house plans and even Victoria's new partnership with Cord. Victoria had fixed them drinks. He had poured seconds while she was involved in explaining her plans for the landscaping she would be designing for his home. He could remember for certain at least one more bourbon.

James shook his head to clear it and immediately regretted the gesture. Remembering the night before was nearly impossible between the pounding in his head and the thudding on the door. One he couldn't do anything about, but the other he could stop.

"This is getting to be a habit," he groaned as he stumbled to his feet. His discomfort intensified, but he ignored it. "I'm coming," he muttered irritably. He jerked open the door and almost got run over by a furious human freight train.

James stared at Cord, working on functioning normally. "Cord? What the devil are you doing here?"

Cord glared at him, his hands clenched into very businesslike fists. "That's my question, and you'd better have a damn good answer."

"Don't shout." James leaned gingerly against the doorjamb and tried to think. Unless he read the signs wrong, he was in serious danger of getting at least one black eye. "It is not what you're thinking. I didn't touch her. The only thing I had my hands on was a glass. Drowning my sorrows." He exaggerated a little for a good cause. Survival. His. "Victoria was nice enough to lend me a bed. Not hers," he added hastily as Cord looked ready to jump him. He might feel like dying at the moment, but he still retained enough reasoning power to tell that Cord wasn't as indifferent to Victoria as he had supposed.

"I like Victoria very much, but I'm only interested in one woman. And as soon as I can pull myself together, I'm going after her." If he had been thinking properly, he probably wouldn't have made such a claim. But having done so, he wasn't about to back down.

Cord took a step closer. Victoria rushed out, reading the scene all wrong. Cord swung around, his temper finding a new target in a spate of hot words. Victoria gave as good as she got. James stood in the middle of the confusion and wished he had a large glass of tomato juice and two aspirin, a quiet bed and sane friends. He had never known being in love was so hazardous to one's health and sanity.

"I'm going."

Neither one paid the least attention to him. Shrugging, he wandered down the hall to find his clothes. Cord and Victoria would have to sort out their own problems without his help. He had more important business to take care of.

Suzanne was back. And he was going to see her tonight. He wanted to hear it from her lips that she wanted Benny and not him. He wanted to see her face when she told him it was over. But more than that, he would tell her the things he should have told her when they were together. And when he was done, he would make love to her and they would burn together one more time. A finish to what was, or a step into what would be.

Ten

"I wish you would sit down. You're making me nervous."

Benny watched Suzanne pace her living room as they waited for Rick's call. While Rick had been able to tell them that Danfield was in the area, he as yet had not been able to pinpoint exactly where.

"You've never been nervous a day in your life." Suzanne turned away from the window, her mind not on Benny or the job. James held all her thoughts since the moment she had seen him with the brunette. A sleepless night hadn't dimmed the image or decreased her sense of betrayal.

"Stupid of me, but I just didn't expect to see him with another woman, in spite of the way we parted and what we made sure he believed. Somehow I thought he'd wait."

Benny got to his feet and went to her. She would never ask for comfort, but she needed it badly. He took her in his arms and held her. She had lost weight over the weeks. It showed in her face and the fragility of her figure.

"I'll grant you the situation looked bad, but he could have had any number of reasons for being with her. Besides, as good-looking as she is she can't hold a candle to you."

"That's your opinion; it didn't look like it was his. He never bent over me like that, as though he were protecting me from something or someone."

"You aren't the kind of woman to want that," Benny pointed out bluntly. "Also, I doubt you have given him much of an opportunity to see any side of your personality but the calm, controlled image you project."

"Maybe." She pulled away from him, not able to tolerate his touch simply because he wasn't James. "I shouldn't be complaining. I made my bed by letting him think we were lovers. I didn't leave him much, not even his pride. He had every right to find himself another woman."

Benny started to comment, but the phone rang. "Yes, Rick. Good. Two hours. Can you make it?" He listened for a second, frowning more deeply with every word. Finally he hung up.

"Well?" Suzanne sat down and forced herself to concentrate. She knew from Benny's face she wasn't going to like whatever Rick had said.

"It seems our friend Danfield's real name is Worrinham. For fifteen years he's been feeding our people to his employers. Only they got greedy, and so did he. Took too much too often. Now he's off to a villa in Argentina with three million dollars in his hot little pockets." Benny swore and slammed his fist into the cushion at the back of the chair. "I want that guy so bad I can taste it."

"How about backup?"

Benny glanced at her. "It's still just you, me and Rick."

Suzanne sighed deeply. She'd been afraid of that. "I was hoping Rick would have us covered by now."

"He would have except the damn records of our people have been doctored. All the available field personnel listed as being here are really elsewhere. God only knows their true positions." Benny raked his fingers through his hair. "And I'll bet my last bonus that Worrinham or Danfield or whatever he calls himself has his place guarded better than Fort Knox."

What couldn't be changed had to be accepted. "So? It won't be the first time we've been outnumbered." At this point in her life she wasn't too worried about the consequences of anything. She had never felt less in control of her destiny.

"This one could be our last. I don't like the sounds of this. It could be a trap."

Suzanne got to her feet. She trusted Benny's instincts, but she wanted this over, trap or no trap. "We don't have a choice, my friend. The rule is we take care of our own. No calling for help. We go with what we've got." She disappeared into the bedroom and reappeared a few moments later dressed all in black. A small deceptively innocent-looking automatic was nestled in the small of her back. A knife handle made a tiny bulge from one high-top shoe.

"I'm ready." She looked Benny over. He was dressed in almost identical fashion. The only difference lay in the size of the gun he carried and the fact that he had made his knife himself, a hobby that could have earned him an enviable reputation.

"Rick will meet us there." He turned out the lights before opening the door.

A quarter moon illuminated their way and also outlined them for the man just coming up the walk. James froze, hearing their whispers before he saw them. Fading into the trees before he thought, he watched Benny stop Suzanne with a hand on her arm. The solid black outfits that both wore took a moment to make their significance felt. He knew what he was looking at. The weapons were noted as his mouth tightened in anger and disbelief.

"I don't want you taking any chances tonight. We want this guy, but not at the cost of your life. He's betrayed enough of us," Benny warned, not liking the reckless gleam in her eyes.

"I'm not a fool," Suzanne returned, angry at the implication.

"You also aren't as nerveless as you used to be," he returned coolly.

James could hear the exchange clearly. His stomach tied into knots. Whatever lay between Benny and Suzanne physically, it was obvious that, in this, Benny was the leader.

"You're just worried because we don't have the manpower. I can hold up my end of the operation."

"Damn straight I'm worried. Even one more man would be better than just three."

James stepped out of the trees, startling them. He had heard too much and not enough. Both whirled in almost identical crouches. "I'm volunteering," he murmured, speaking only to Benny. He wasn't ready to face Suzanne. His anger needed an outlet, but not here and not now.

"No!" Suzanne shook her head, taking a step forward to place herself between the two men. Benny caught her arm before she could take her position.

"You don't know what you're getting into." Benny studied James. "You don't even know if we're the good guys."

James's smile wasn't nice or pretty. "You're not the only one who can ask questions or follow leads. I don't know exactly who you work for, but I do have an idea. You know I can do the work, don't you. Three years of intelligence work for the military isn't the same as this but it did teach me a few tricks that should be useful. Whatever check you ran on me should have told you that at least."

Benny nodded, ignoring Suzanne. "That was a while back."

"Some things you don't forget."

The conversation made too much sense to Suzanne. Benny had had James investigated and hadn't told her. Now there were two betrayals not one. "I won't have it," Suzanne interjected. "I don't know what you found out about James, Benny." She paused to glare at her partner. "But you won't involve him in this."

"Shut up, Suzanne. I'll deal with you later," James said harshly.

She swung around, her eyes narrowing at James's implacable tone. If she shut her eyes, she could still see that brunette in his arms. Jealousy, rage and hurt were a potent combination. "You and whose army?"

James ignored her. He was so infuriated he knew that if he started, he would not finish in a hurry. She looked beautiful, weary, fragile, and yet strong. She faced him in the darkness, her eyes glittering with temper and frustration. Her body was taut with anger and tension. He wasn't sure whether he wanted to take her in his arms and love her through the night or spank her tail for not trusting him enough to tell him what she and Benny were involved in.

"How long do we have?"

Suzanne inhaled sharply at the snub. Neither man was listening. The feeling of being left in the dark was a new one and she didn't like it. Only the fact they had a job to do kept her in place.

"Less than two hours to get ten miles north and set up." Benny gestured toward Suzanne's light-colored BMW. "Let's get going."

James shook his head. "Let's take mine. It's black. No sense in advertising our presence if someone is watching the roads. Good thing I wore jeans and a dark shirt."

Both men started for James's Ferrari. Somehow Suzanne found herself sandwiched between the two men. Her shoulders brushed James's as they walked. She tried without success to pretend the contact didn't exist. His glance mocked her efforts. Their gazes held.

In his eyes she read fury, hurt and a recklessness she hadn't expected she'd ever know. Suddenly the man she thought she knew was gone, replaced by a sharp-eyed shadow that moved beside her without making a sound. He was dangerous, she realized in shock. This was no shrewd businessman now, rather a hunter who was Benny's equal and maybe a shade better. She could feel the energy being channeled through him, the anticipation, the lack of fear.

"I'll ride in the back," she muttered, unnerved by her discoveries. She yanked open the door and got in before either man could object.

"It won't help," James murmured against her ear. He slipped by her to get into the driver's seat without waiting for an answer.

Suzanne stared at the back of his head, fighting her emotions and the exhaustion pulling at her body. She only had to hold together one more night. Danfield was close. The job was almost done. She couldn't afford James. He was draining her will and making her wonder if her judgment had been so wrong that she could have fallen in love with a man that she didn't know.

"Where to?"

"Take Interstate 190 north out of the city. We're heading for a place called Clifton. Do you know it?"

He nodded. "Now fill me in. If I'm going hunting I want to know who and why."

Benny leaned back in the seat, considering just how much to tell him. He could legitimately refuse to part with any information. He didn't think that James would back out, simply because Suzanne was involved. Yet he respected the man and the feeling he had for his woman too much not to be honest.

"I don't need to tell you that this can go no further."

"You don't."

"About three and a half years ago, one of the groups I work for called me in to talk about a rather strange occurrence. A certain sector was showing a high mortality rate in a line that shouldn't be that risky. Couriers do not normally get removed. There are easier ways." He frowned as he remembered the statistics. "Anyway, I was temporarily reassigned. Not a problem, because I had begun my work in that sector anyway. Suzanne and I became partners of a sort. Nothing surfaced for a long time no matter how hard I looked. Finally, I heard there was a target list out. My name was first, then hers. Somebody had gotten worried. I had touched something, but I didn't know what. I'm a stubborn cuss and I like living. So I faked my own demise to get myself some room to maneuver. I made it clear before I did the deed that I was working strictly solo. Left Suzanne in the clear, especially when I kind of set her up as being the indirect cause of my passing."

James tensed, his fingers biting into the leather-wrapped steering wheel. Despite knowing Suzanne had lied to him about a lot of things, he had a small measure of her personality. It didn't take much thinking to know what being involved in Benny's death would have done to her. Compassion and sympathy for her feelings sat ill with the anger that still raged inside him.

He shifted in his seat, darting a glance in the rearview mirror.

"Suzanne quit. She couldn't—"

"You don't need to go into what I could or couldn't do," Suzanne interrupted from the back seat. She didn't want that time in her life discussed when she hadn't really had time to come to terms with it herself. She could feel James's gaze on her, but she didn't look his way. She couldn't handle seeing his anger and still hang on to her composure.

Benny glanced at her, reading her distress.

She stared him down, knowing he didn't agree with her reluctance.

He turned away and picked up his story. "Anyway, to make a long story short, it has taken me three years to run Danfield to the ground. This guy is clever. He's set us all up, and if his greed hadn't gotten in the way, he might still be doing it. That's when and why I approached Suzanne. I had finally narrowed the field of suspects to two. The problem was both were in positions that meant quite a number of our people could have been involved. I couldn't trust the regular routes. Suzanne was my choice. I didn't count on busting up her life, and I damn well didn't count on Danfield realizing that I had him all but trussed up. When he ran, we had to change our plans from the trap I had intended to spring to hunting him out. We've been down a bunch of blind trails since we left town. But we have him now if we move fast enough. He's on his way out of the country, this time with his money and sanctuary. If we had had the time, I could have mounted a full-scale net, but as it is we're all we've got." He gestured toward the side road ahead. "Turn here."

James eased down the dirt road, cutting his headlights to rely on the parking lights.

"You do remember a lot," Benny murmured, appreciating the move.

James ignored the compliment and focused on the necessities. "I need a weapon, the layout and the plan."

"There are four of us and, as far as we know, eight people in the house. Along with three Dobies."

"Cute," James muttered grimly. "Who gets the dogs?"

"I do," Suzanne inserted, edging forward on the seat. It was time she took an active part in the conversation. The goal was in sight.

"No way. Men are easier to handle than animals. I'll do it."

Suzanne pulled a small gun from her pocket. "There isn't much danger. I'm simply going to tranquilize them."

"For a hasty plan, you come well prepared." James glanced at the dart gun and then at her face. No emotion was visible in her expression or her eyes. Both were cool, empty and, to the unenlightened, calm. He knew better. He could feel the energy flowing through her, almost taste her anticipation. She was like a high-strung racehorse standing in the starting gate. And he had thought her gentle, soft. Fool. The control he had admired was still there, but with more strength than he could ever have imagined. Once again he felt the stirring of anger that she had chosen to hide this part of herself from him. She hadn't trusted him and that hurt.

"Park here."

Benny's voice pulled him back to the present. Exerting his own control, he concentrated on the job at hand. A slip here would cost one of them dearly. They got out and were joined by another man.

"Who's this?" Rick demanded, eyeing James suspiciously.

"One of us." Benny stared at the large house partially hidden by the trees. About three hundred yards away, it looked like many of the old Southern homes that peppered the area. White columns, a long veranda and the impression of a graceful, long-gone era. The one jarring note was the chain link fence about the grounds and the strategic placement of spotlights.

"Damn! Looks like he's expecting company." Rick squatted on his haunches.

James slipped into the shadows of the trees, instincts he thought gone reasserting themselves. "Three guards, two with dogs," he whispered to himself.

"One dog is probably free," Suzanne murmured, her eyes, too, on the house. When she had seen him move away from Rick and Benny, she had followed without being sure why.

James turned to look at her. The filtered moonlight silvered her skin, tracing the lines with gentle fingers of light. "How long were you in the business?"

The reasons for not telling him were gone. "Six years."

"Guilt made you quit." He glanced back at the house without waiting for a reply. Would she go back, given the chance? He wanted to ask and didn't.

Suzanne stared at his face. Had she lost him? The question trembled on her tongue, but she didn't ask. Benny joined them.

"Rick and I will take the back. You and Suzanne can handle the front." He handed James a paper containing a line drawing of the house's interior. "The meeting place is marked. Don't take any chances. All we want is Danfield."

"I'd rather go with you," Suzanne objected, touching Benny's arm.

He shook his head without looking at her. "Not your choice, love. Or mine. You may not know why he's here, but I do." He grinned before touching two fingers to his forehead and melting into the darkness without a sound.

"Let's go. I lead, you follow." James moved off before she could object.

Suzanne wasted a second and a glare before matching his pace. She owed Benny for this, and she always collected her debts. They ran into the Doberman the moment they cut through the fence. One dart stopped the animal without permanent damage. There was little cover to be found between the fence and the house, but James made good use of what there was. They reached the veranda and took out the two guards and their dogs walking the grounds, with a sleeping dart each. It was almost too easy. Instincts on ready, Suzanne tensed. Danfield was too smart for his home ground to be so easily breached.

"Too simple," she muttered.

"I know." James crouched beside the front door. "I'll bet you any amount of money that we've tripped a few silent alarms. Probably a light grid."

Suzanne studied the porch. Any of the windows could be used as points of entry. "Diversion?"

"No time."

"Go in at the same time, different ways."

"Logical but risky."

She recognized his hesitation then and was angered by it. "I can take care of myself. Don't soft-pedal for me. I don't need a shield," she whispered with stinging emphasis.

James clenched his teeth against an explosion of his own. She might be right, but it didn't make what they had to do any easier to handle. He pointed to the floor-length window to his left. "You take that one and I'll hit this one." He caught her arm when she would have moved away. Yanking her against him, he kissed her hard and deep. It didn't matter that she didn't respond or that they were both angry. All that mattered was holding her in his arms one more time. "Silently. Now go!" he commanded, pushing her toward the window.

Suzanne went, her lips still tingling from his possession. It was a measure of her control and training that her fingers worked the lock with steady precision. She edged through the opening with almost no sound. Not so James. The front door shattered with a well-placed foot.

"No!" Face white, Suzanne rushed through the study. James had made himself a target as cover for the rest of them. Two shots from the back of the house made her draw her gun. She reached the door just as it slammed open, knocking the breath from her body and the weapon from her hand. Danfield, wild-eyed and desperate, stared at her for a split second before grabbing her by the hair and jerking her in front of him like a shield. Suzanne struggled once then ceased as his arm tightened around her throat and the gun pressed against her temple.

Benny met James in the hall. "Rick's got his hands full in back. Where's Suzanne?"

"The study. Danfield's there."

One ugly oath.

"My feelings exactly." James eased down the hall. "If he hurts her—" He broke off as Danfield came out of the room, dragging Suzanne with him.

Suzanne stared at James, knowing he was poised on the knife-edge of action. The arm on her throat tightened. She didn't notice. Her whole being was caught in the mesh of danger to James. She had thought to protect him from this. And he had thought to protect her. Neither of them had succeeded.

"I'll kill her," Danfield threatened.

"Then you won't have your shield." Benny edged closer.

"I mean it," he screamed, beginning to panic.

"You don't have any escape. We're not letting you leave with her."

"She's your partner."

"She left me for dead." Cold, precise words, none betraying the agony of watching that gun press against Suzanne's face.

Danfield stared, reading truth in lies. He turned to James almost wildly. "Tell him I'll do it. She's your woman. I'll shoot her. I will."

James shrugged. "You're behind the times. She was my woman until she took another man."

Suzanne could feel the trembling in the arm holding her. One more push and then they might have him. "You picked the wrong person to use. The only reason any of us are here together is because you made sure that the rest of our people were unavailable."

"You're lying." He glanced at her face.

It was the slip in concentration that James and Benny had been waiting for. James hit him high, yanking his gun hand up and away. Benny snatched Suzanne away as the weapon discharged. One punch and Danfield folded like a used tent against the wall, sliding down into an unconscious heap.

James turned to Benny. "Is she all right?"

"Missing hair. Nothing else."

"Don't talk about me as if I'm not here," Suzanne snapped, angry at herself for having let Danfield use her.

James closed the space between them in three strides. Catching her shoulders, he whirled her to face him. One look at her wide eyes and the traces of fear still lingering there stilled his tongue. He dropped his hands.

"I'm going to help Rick. I'll be back in a minute."

Suzanne stared after him, shocked at the rage and then the sudden blanking of his expression. "I don't understand."

"You'd better start." Benny reached over to snap a set of cuffs on Danfield. "That man is ready to explode. I don't know how he's held off this long. I also wouldn't want to be in your shoes for all the tea in China."

"He has no right."

"If you think that, then you haven't the brains I've always credited you with. You gave him the right when you took him to your bed. You've lied to him and you haven't trusted him, and I have an idea that matters to him a lot. It would to me."

"You know why."

"I know why you told me, but I don't think that was the real reason." He headed for the phone. "I'm going back with Rick. You and James can ride to town together."

"You're leaving me with him?"

Benny grinned, looking thoroughly masculine in his amusement. "Honey, I couldn't keep you with me tonight if I tried. And I like my head too much to attempt to get between that man and you. You're on your own."

"Traitor," she accused, meaning the word. "I'm not ready for this." She spread her hands, pleading as she had never done before.

Benny watched her, wishing he could help and knowing he couldn't. "Are you afraid of him?"

"No. I don't know. He wouldn't hurt me physically, but..."

"There are worse ways," he finished for her. He touched her cheek. "Then tell him to leave and mean it. He isn't the type to force himself into your life."

Suzanne looked away from his knowing eyes. "Maybe I wish he were. Maybe I need to see him out of control. Maybe I need to know he won't hate me if I can't be the calm, poised woman he said he admired in me." The confusion of emotions prompted the words.

James reentered the hall to find them standing close together. Jealousy raged in his eyes as he spoke. He still didn't know if they were or had been lovers. "I'm taking Suzanne back to town."

Benny glanced at him, reading the emotion James held in check. Benny didn't agree with Suzanne. He definitely didn't want to see this man out of control. Ever. "I'd planned on going with Rick anyway."

Eleven

———

I'm not going with you." Suzanne stood immovable in the middle of the study, facing James. She met his blazing eyes, defying him to make her.

"Afraid?" he challenged her.

The lie came from more than pride. "No. We just don't have anything to talk about." She shrugged, still watching him warily. Something about the way he stood there worried her. Control. She hated it in him when her own was hanging by a thread. Didn't he see that to talk now in the aftermath of the adrenaline surge would gain nothing but out-of-control emotions and words better left unsaid? She edged toward the door. If she could just get out. Benny wouldn't really leave her behind.

James moved when she moved, knowing he wasn't

going to let her walk away from him again. Once in his lifetime was enough. "We're going to talk."

"Tomorrow." Desperation lent sharpness to her voice.

"Tonight." He stalked closer, crowding her but not caring.

She could see he wasn't going to be denied. The strength of purpose in the way he mirrored her actions was awesome. She wanted to run but there was no place to go. She wanted to scream but was afraid of even that. She loved James. But he cared only for the calm, poised woman she had made herself be. And even that was gone, for now there was another in her place. Defeat. A new feeling rushed through her, taking her anger. Her shoulders slumped as she turned toward the door. He followed her to the car without speaking. The drive back to town was equally silent. Expecting him to go to her apartment, she was surprised to discover him parking in the underground garage of his place.

"Don't bother fighting me about going upstairs," James warned when she made no move to open the car door. "We are going to talk."

The hard tone coupled with the no-win nature of the situation snapped Suzanne out of her apathy. Temper surged through her, flashing in her eyes and in the sharp movements of her body as she got out of the car.

"You're learning," he said roughly.

"Don't push." She sent him a glance of dislike as she entered the elevator ahead of him.

He ignored it. All he wanted was privacy and time. She had walked out on him. He had to have answers no matter how hard they might be to accept.

They entered the apartment, Suzanne going across the room to stand at the windows overlooking the city. James leaned against the door and watched her stiff back. He waited for her to speak. The silence lengthened.

Suzanne braced herself for a barrage of questions. They didn't come. She glanced over her shoulder when she couldn't stand the waiting any longer.

As if it were the signal he had been looking for, James spoke. "Why?"

"Why what?"

"Why did you leave like that? You had to know that I wouldn't sit calmly by. That I would check with Pat, if no one else. You had to know what I would think when I discovered you left with Benny. What did I ever do to deserve that?"

"I didn't think about you looking for me." Suzanne watched him flinch at the truth, hating herself for hurting him but remembering too well the black-haired woman in the restaurant.

"Damn you." His hands clenched against the emotion roiling within.

"No. Damn you." Suzanne took a step closer, jealousy eating away the last of her control. "Who was she? It didn't take you long to fill my side of the bed." The pain and the anger mixed in the harsh words.

He glared at her. "I took no woman to bed, you crazy fool. Even when I thought you had gone off with

Benny without caring enough to tell me to my face that you chose him, I didn't look for someone else.''

"Then who was she?"

"A friend. A woman in love with a man who didn't think she was ready for love. I held her hand and she held mine.'' He raked his fingers through his hair. "Tell me about Benny."

"I told you."

"No, you didn't. He did. You didn't trust me enough to tell me anything.'' The knowledge of the lies she had told him hurt.

"How could I?" She paced the floor, caught by the truth. "Do you think I wanted to lie to you? I hate lies because I have lived with them too long. But you didn't want what I really was. I couldn't tell you that I have carried a gun and knew how to use it. I couldn't tell you that shadows and danger are as familiar to me as this apartment is to you. I couldn't tell you that the t'ai chi that your niece practices has saved my life a time or two and maybe even hers on that one night that seems a lifetime ago. Would you have believed me? Would you have wanted to know me, really know me, beyond the bedroom and the desire? I attract you. I know that. But I didn't think it was more than the woman I pretended to be. I tried to be sure. I tried to fight my attraction to you, but you won. I gave you more than I have given anyone before you, and yet I gave you less. I knew that one day I would have to face you. I didn't expect it to be when I was caught in the middle of my past. I didn't expect Benny to rise from the dead. I didn't want you hurt, damn it. I wanted you safe. You weren't made for this, I thought. I tried to protect you, knowing I would have to hurt you to do it. I was wrong. But I would do it again, because you gave me no other choice. You never looked beyond that which you could see."

Two strides brought him in front of her. He caught her shoulders, staring into her eyes. "And whose fault was that? You never let me see the real you. Except maybe once. That night we made love as if there were no tomorrow. That was the only honesty in you." He glared at her. "I never cheated you. But you cheated me."

"I had no choice." The tears stood in her eyes as she faced him. Why couldn't he understand? "Benny's death hurt me. I ran because I needed to hide. I came here and built a new place, a different place for a different woman." She jerked out of his hands. "What's the use? I'm a stranger to you now. I do things that women don't usually do. You wanted one kind of lover and got an illusion." She laughed harshly. "You weren't the only one who got cheated. I wanted to tell you so many times. You have no idea how hard it was not to let go when we loved." She yelped as the room spun. "Put me down."

James didn't know what was truth or lie anymore. The rational part of him understood her words, but his hurt went too deep to forgive or accept so easily. "Be quiet. I want truth. I want an end to this illusion as you call it. You can't lie to me here." He dropped her in the middle of the bed, coming down beside her before she could scramble away. "Words can mean anything, but bodies, our bodies, don't lie."

"This isn't going to solve anything," she protested, slapping at his hands as he yanked her black sweater over her head.

Her breasts glowed softly above the flimsy lace bra. James cradled the soft mounds, his thumbs teasing the nipples through the mesh. Suzanne bit back a moan of desire as she tried to twist away. James threw a leg over her thighs and trapped her in place.

"I won't let you do this to me."

"To us." James stared into her eyes. "You want me still. I want you. Deny it."

Suzanne opened her lips to say the words. "I can't." The tears slipped down her temple to dampen her hair. "But it isn't me you want...."

He bent his head and stole the rest of her words, words neither of them needed to hear again. "It's you I'm holding in my arms. Your red hair is on fire, and the heat of your body is calling to the heat in mine. Your scent is in my mind, and I can still taste your lips on my tongue. What more do I need?"

No woman could stand against a strong man's honest need. Suzanne lost the battle before it had begun. With a soft sigh she lifted her arms to his neck, pulling him down to her. "The other one. Was she really a friend?" She had to be sure.

"Only that." He slipped a hand beneath her to free the bra.

Suzanne unbuttoned his shirt, her fingers tangling in the hair on his chest. "I had dreams of this," she admitted huskily. "So little sleep, but when I did, dreams of you waited."

He looked in her eyes and read the torment of their parting. She spoke of need and wanting, but never of love. He wondered if she even knew what it meant. Strangers, she called them. Strangers they were, yet lovers still. "Mine were nightmares. Lonely, unending nightmares of you in his arms." He rolled onto her, needing to imprint his body on hers.

"Never that. Friend only and partner." She inhaled the scent of him, letting the memories fill her mind. Now it was safe to recall their passion. Now she wanted to remember, to feel, to hope even if it too were an illusion.

His lips touched hers, the desire sizzling in the single gesture, ripping the civilized veneer from his mind. His hands tightened on her body, taking, wanting, needing with every instinct man had ever known. His woman. Whatever went before or after would never change this time now.

"I trusted you," he breathed angrily as he stripped the jeans from her. His own followed in impatient movements.

"I couldn't tell you." A plea, never made to anyone else but to him. She met life as she found it, asking no quarter. For him she would have begged and still understood when he could not give. She loved though she would not tell him. Love was a burden when not returned.

His hands framed her face as she saw him search her eyes. She stared back at him. "Make love to me?" she asked. She risked rejection to take the pain of the moment he had found she had left with Benny from his mind. She couldn't take back the illusion, the lies, but she could offer him a way to even the score.

"All night if that's what you want." He joined their bodies in a single thrust, ignoring foreplay for the need to mate. She met him with the same strength and determination. Arching to deepen his joining, accepting him and his needs, giving back passion and softness.

His hands flexed on her flesh, his fingers kneading her body, stroking, pleasuring, lighting fires with every touch. Suzanne's breath caught at the intensity of his expression, the almost savage look of arousal. The skin was pulled tight across his cheekbones, his jaw and mouth set as though he were in pain. She had wanted to see him out of control. She had her wish.

Her hands trembled on his chest as her entire body quivered in reaction to the fierce male hunger. Heat rose in her, melting her, unraveling her until the deepest inner core was visible. He touched her breasts, cupping the fullness to lift them to his mouth. His lips closed on the tips, sucking, pulling, biting gently until Suzanne knew the sweet pain of desire. It filled her, forcing moans to her lips, moans he tasted as nectar from heaven. His hips moved, deepening the union. Sweat stood on his brow at the restraint he imposed. He wanted her in every part of his being. He wanted her to know that she belonged to him, that no other man could satisfy her the way he could. He wanted to wipe the images of lovers past forever from her mind.

"Take it all," he groaned, demanded, pleaded. He hung over her, his expression exquisitely tormented.

The primitive chant washed over her, and she cried out again as he moved in and out, powerfully, in-

escapably. It had never been like this for her, so pain-
fully intense that it was unbearable. She had never
been loved this way before, knowing that her breath
would still forever and her heart would stop marking
time if anything ever happened to him. If this was all
he wanted of her, then she would give herself freely
and completely, branding him with her passion. If he
wanted only the illusion, she would learn to live with
it.

He rolled his hips in a heavy surge. It was too much
pleasure, too much desire. Her senses crested, shattered. She gasped and cried out, writhing beneath him
until he caught fire, too. She couldn't see, couldn't
breathe, could only feel. He came to her, retreating
and then coming again. She tried to hold him, to beg
him to push them over the edge. Her body betrayed
her, for her strength was gone. She could only give and
give and give. Her name was on his lips as he thrust
forward and upward in one giant push to the last peak.
She rose to meet him, crying his name.

They collapsed together, breathing heavily, damp
with love and perspiration. The silence closed around
them, deep, endless as the hour before dawn. Sleep
crept over Suzanne, the true rest that the weeks of
separation had denied her. Her lashes drifted shut, and
still she held him as though she could not let him go.

James felt her body relax, her breathing deepen. He
rolled onto his back, taking her with him. Separation
was unthinkable. Tomorrow they would talk. Nothing had been settled. But for now he held her.

Suzanne awoke slowly, conscious of a feeling of well-being and warmth. The weight across her breasts created a sensation of safety rather than entrapment. She turned her head, staring at James's sleeping face. The gentle sunlight of the morning touched him with gold. She studied him, seeing the strength that even the defenselessness of slumber could not steal. She wanted to touch him, to rekindle the passion that had swept all before its path the night before. Her fingers clenched to trap the urge before it became action. She would give him anything he asked while he held her, but she could not let herself be weakened. He still spoke only of want, not of love. Love could forgive her lies, but want would try and fail. She had no life. Her illusion was gone. She could offer him nothing even had he loved her. She had faced that knowledge when Benny had come back into her life. She didn't know what she was anymore. She had thought her life set. For very different reasons Benny and James had shown her it was not.

The danger. Once her reason for existing, the high of beating the odds no longer held its magic or its temptation. Yet the careful way she lived in New Orleans felt like an ill-fitting glove now. Her past and her present were overlapping, filling gaps and creating conflict. She didn't know what she wanted to do with her life. What she could do. Her business and her home still waited. Did her man?

Her eyes traced his features. How did he want her? He had asked her to move in with him. Was it enough? Could she make it enough? Last night she had thought so. Now, lying here beside him, remembering the woman in the restaurant, she knew she had lied. She hadn't expected the violent surge of jealousy. She hadn't expected to need him. She had never needed anyone. Restless, angry with herself for having no answers, she slipped from the bed. She couldn't stay. James would wake soon. She couldn't face him until she knew what she really wanted and needed. Moving silently, she dressed and let herself out of the apartment. With no car and no money, she had to walk home.

It was miles away. Four, to be exact. The city was just rising to meet another day. She watched the process without really seeing it. The paper carriers made their deliveries. The street artists set up for a day of commerce. No one bothered her, the figure dressed in black, though many noted her passing. She paused at her street corner, looking at the house she had made into the first home she had known. Where was the feeling of security and peace that had once filled her at this sight? She sighed, realizing that it too was an illusion.

Even when she entered the apartment, the feeling of displacement continued. A shower didn't help, nor did the breakfast that she barely touched. She walked through the rooms, touching things she had gathered in her travels, reliving scenes, many better left forgotten. It was during her second circuit that she realized she was waiting, waiting for James. He would come after her. She knew it as surely as she breathed.

"Fool!" She whirled around, finally pushed to the edge. Grabbing her car keys, she left the apartment. She would not force him to make the decision for her. She would find her own answers. But first she would lay the past to rest. And for that, she needed to see Benny. The streets were almost empty, so the drive to his hotel was short. It took three sharp raps on the door before she could get an answer and then it was a grumpy demand.

"Suzanne," she snapped, in no mood to pander to his slow-to-wake-up mode.

Benny pulled on a robe and stumbled to the door. "If you didn't bring any coffee with you, go out and come in again."

"I didn't bring any coffee, and you aren't going to need it anyway." Suzanne tossed her handbag on the bed and took the only chair in the room.

Benny eyed her, recognizing the expression on her face too well. When she lost her temper, there was really no place a sane man could hide. Better to ride the storm. He blinked and forced his sluggish brain into high gear. He had been expecting an explosion for a while. But he would have thought James would be the one to trigger it.

"I didn't expect you this morning," he murmured, offering her a target before she could work up a full head of steam.

Suzanne glared at him. "You mean you didn't expect me at all after you threw me to the wolf last night."

"Technically, it was this morning."

"Technically, you're lucky you still have a head. Don't push it," she returned mockingly.

He grimaced. Maybe he should have thought twice about offering himself up on the sacrificial altar for another man. "I thought you would be pleased. I know how you hate paperwork."

"In a pig's eye. You figured you men should stick together. I could wring your neck for that stunt. It's my life and you had no business messing in it."

"Somebody had to. You probably would have convinced yourself that you should leave, or act like a noble little female or some other such rot. I know you, remember. I know all those little idealistic tendencies. Heaven knows, I've bumped my knees on enough of your scruples." He dropped onto the bed, punching the pillows so that he could sit up and still be comfortable. "You wouldn't have gone to him after seeing him with that woman, whoever she is."

"No, I wouldn't have," she agreed. "I thought he had made his choice."

"On erroneous information. But you wouldn't have wanted to risk hurting him to try and straighten out the lies." He shook his head. "Sometimes I don't know how you survive with that sense of fair play still intact. Don't you know all is fair in love and war?"

"Who said anything about love?"

"I did. It's written all over your face. And his."

"Mine, maybe. His, no. Desire. You should know about that."

"Low blow. And you're wrong."

"He said nothing."

"Knowing you, you gave him no chance. Besides, after everything that's happened, maybe he's afraid to tell you how he feels."

"James is afraid of nothing. Least of all, me."

Benny stared at her, a grin slowly forming on his lips. "Have you got it bad!" He chuckled, liking the idea. "I've watched you handle stuff that would make me think twice without turning a hair, and falling in love has you stymied."

Anger was too close a companion to handle even his gentle amusement. Suzanne knew a number of ways to retaliate. It was a measure of her confusion that she chose snatching one of the pillows from beneath his head and smacking him with it before he could protect himself.

At that moment the door quickly opened. James stood on the threshold, glaring at them impartially. "I wonder why I'm not surprised to find her here with you. I woke up this morning expecting to talk to my woman and what do I find? An armful of sweet loving? A soft kiss? Maybe breakfast or coffee? Oh, no. An empty, cold bed." With each question, he took a step closer. "She wouldn't have just walked out, I assured myself. Not this time." He studied their frozen positions with clinical interest. "And when I finally realized that you really had gone, I figured you needed some time at home alone. It nearly killed me, but I didn't rush out after you. I showered, dressed and ate—not much, I'll admit."

Suzanne roused herself enough to let go of the pillow and to straighten up. The anger emanating from him was intimidating. She had a feeling that the next few minutes were going to be very sticky indeed. "I was com—"

"I would be quiet if I were you," James suggested in a mild voice. "I also think I would move away from that bed. For his sake and yours." He tipped his head. "I think I told you before that I'm a jealous man, a very jealous man," he added when she showed a bit too much tardiness in following his suggestion.

Suzanne moved. So did Benny, stifling a deeper grin. "Don't pick on me. I'm an innocent by-stander." He held up his hands, palms out, realizing once again that he liked this man. "I've got one question."

James glanced at him, seeing the grin, knowing the cause and ignoring both. He didn't give a damn what anyone thought anymore. "What?"

"Do you like Scotch?"

"In my worse moments, it's the only thing to drink."

Suzanne felt like hitting them both. "I will not have this. If you've got something to say—"

James swung his head to look at her as she lifted her chin to glare at him. "I have something to say all right, and you're going to stay long enough to listen this time, and we're not going to end up in bed before we talk, either."

For the first time in her life, Suzanne blushed. "James, what's gotten into you? You didn't need to add that last part, not in front of him, at least."

"There is no him."

She glanced around, realizing James spoke the truth. Benny had disappeared into the bathroom, the door shut behind him.

"It's just you and me. Now you have two choices. You can walk out of this hotel with me, or I can carry you out." He watched her, purpose in every line of his body.

"You wouldn't dare."

He smiled then, almost as though he had been waiting for just that statement. "Wrong words. Right choice."

Before she could protest, Suzanne found herself slung over his shoulder like a sack of potatoes. Outraged, she started wiggling to get free. "Put me down, you big bully. I'll wring your neck when I get my hands on you."

James laughed as he hooked an arm across the back of her knees.

"I'll send you two cases of Scotch for the wedding. Don't start without me," Benny called from behind the door.

"I'll string you both up," Suzanne threatened on the way out of the room.

Twelve

I'll never forgive you for this," Suzanne said angrily. Hanging upside down was not having a beneficial effect on her temper. Her hair was in her face. She knew too well the sight she presented, slung over his shoulder, and she couldn't even get leverage enough to retaliate. Grabbing her hair, she managed to deal with at least one of her problems and wished she hadn't when she stared at the three older women standing in the elevator goggling at her. Suzanne moaned in embarrassment and tucked her head down in the small of James's back.

James smiled at his audience. He was beginning to enjoy himself. He hadn't realized that giving sway to his impulses and his emotions could enliven his life so much. Strolling through a crowded hotel lobby on a busy weekend with Suzanne hanging down his back wasn't the way he would have chosen to appear in public, but he was beginning to see distinct advantages. For one thing, judging by the unintelligible murmurs coming from behind him, Suzanne would never again dare him to do anything. Of course, her aspersions on his ancestry, while shocking to the people sharing the elevator, did lend a certain flair since Suzanne was managing to be quite creative without losing that wonderful lady-like quality he so admired.

"Really, darling. I'm stunned. I couldn't possibly be related to a camel," he drawled, catching one especially ludicrous comparison. "There aren't any in the South that I know of."

"I'll give you a camel." Suzanne raised her head as the doors to the lobby opened. "I can walk."

"Wouldn't think of it. I don't want you too tired for the wedding."

The words meant nothing to her. "There isn't going to be any wedding."

"You mean you're not going to make an honest man of me after spending the night—"

"James, shut up," she snapped, turning scarlet. There had to be at least fifteen people in the common area. Every one of them had his or her ear glued to the conversation.

James walked out the door to his car standing in the loading zone in front of the hotel. He slipped the parking valet a five before stuffing Suzanne gently into the front seat. "If you try to make a break for it, I promise I'll tie you in," he vowed before bending to kiss her.

If the mention of a wedding, which had finally penetrated her temper enough to be understood, hadn't drained the fight from her, the kiss would have. Hard, fast and deep, it touched all the emotions that raged between them. The uncertainty lost its importance in the deluge of feeling. The future was still unsettled, but at least there was hope.

James got into the car, relieved he had gotten this far. Suzanne was with him now. Whether she remained so would depend on how convincing and understanding he could be. Desire had been born in an illusion, love would be born in truth.

"Where are we going?" Suzanne demanded when it became clear that neither his apartment nor hers was their destination.

"A surprise. Sit back and enjoy the ride."

Suzanne looked at him, the first time she had done so since he had kissed her. His face was an unreadable mask. His hands were relaxed on the wheel. She had seen him many times in just such a pose. Today it hurt not to know what he was thinking.

She had to know. "You said marriage. Did you mean it?"

He glanced at her. "Why would you think I didn't?"

"You never said anything about it before," she persisted. Hope was so easy to give in to and so hard to handle when it died. She couldn't let herself believe in a future.

"How could I? We were playing by different rules then. Why did you think I asked you to move in with me when I had never asked that of another woman in my life?"

"A convenient affair." The knowledge still hurt. Even then, she had not known she wanted more. She had realized living with him would have been torture, but she had thought it was because of the lie she lived.

He laughed shortly. "There is very little convenience about us, or haven't you noticed?" He guided the car onto a dirt road that had been overgrown with trees and weeds until recently. The ride was bumpy, taking all his concentration. He pulled to a stop on a hill.

"Let's walk from here."

Suzanne got out and stood looking around. There was nothing to see in the immediate vicinity. "To where?"

James took her arm and tucked it into his. His hip brushed hers as he urged her over the rough ground. He had wanted to save his surprise. Now he needed it. "To here." He stopped in the shadow of a copse of trees. Land, recently cleared, surveyed and staked, began a few yards away. A foundation, the roof and studs for the walls that were soon to be added gave a hint to the vision Cord had turned into the reality of James's house to be.

"I hope you'll live here with me. Raise a family here. Be my wife and my lover. Grow old with me here." James turned her in his arms. This wasn't the way he had planned his proposal, but he couldn't wait any longer. She was building her defenses higher with every second. He could feel it even if he didn't understand it. She didn't believe he meant marriage and forever. "I'm asking you to marry me."

Suzanne stared into his face, seeing emotions, hope, need, uncertainty and determination. "You can't mean that. You don't really know me. All those things we said last night are still true."

He didn't try to deny the truth. There were more important issues at stake. "There was one thing we never did say. One question I didn't ask. Do you love me?"

She wanted to lie. He asked of her what he himself had not spoken of. She was afraid to be vulnerable first. Marriage did not mean love.

James shook her gently, reading the fear, beginning to understand her better. "I love you. My pride against yours. Is it so very hard to drop the barriers, Suzanne?"

She raised her fingers to touch his lips. Her fingers trembled as she traced their outline. He was stronger than she was. "I don't know me anymore. I thought I did, but Benny and these last few weeks shook up my life. I hurt you and myself. What if I can't stop hurting us? I'm afraid." She leaned against him. His strength wrapped around her. "I could say yes because I do love you." His arms tightened, but he didn't try to stop her speaking. "I loved you enough to try to protect you from my life. I loved you enough to accept an affair because I thought that was all you wanted."

He laid his cheek against her hair. "What do you want, love? Tell me."

"I don't know. I can't go back to the danger. I know that. I don't want it anymore. I also can't go back to being so careful, so cautious. That isn't me and never was. I have a business, and I'm not even sure that I want it anymore."

"But do you want me?"

"Yes." The answer was quick, sharp, firm. No hesitation.

James exhaled a deep sigh. He tilted her head up, seeing the silver trails of tears flowing down her cheeks. "Then that's all that matters. We can handle the rest between us. We've got the best things in the world going for us. Where you're concerned, I have no pride. The proof is in that stupid stunt of hauling you out of Benny's hotel room in front of half the population of New Orleans. And your proof is in the lengths you would go to protect me even if I didn't need it. The question is, are we brave enough to take a flying leap into marriage and worry about the small stuff later. That's the danger, my love. Are you game?"

Suzanne stood in the circle of his arms and weighed the past, present and future. Danger alone. Safety alone. Danger and safety together. No choice. One choice. "Just when is this marriage to take place?" she asked, smiling through the tears. The look of relief and delight on James's face was worth every risk she had ever taken or would take.

"It would be today, but I want to do this thing up right. White gown, attendants, best man to lose the ring and all. Pictures for the mantel and a honeymoon to I-don't-care-where." He kissed her deeply, only raising his head when he needed to breathe. "Say you want the same."

She laughed softly, happily. "With the exception of the white." And before he could protest the change of color, "I look ghastly in white. Ivory is better."

"Long. With a train. A long veil, too."

She blinked. "Whatever for?"

"Tradition. People like us need a little tradition to leaven the quirks in our nature."

"Are you so sure we have quirks? You know more than I do."

He took her arm and started across his land. "You may not see your future, but I do. You like to travel, so we'll do a lot of that. There'll always be something intriguing you can't wait to buy for the shop. I'll curse the customs people, the weight restrictions and the mail. Then you'll get tired of traveling. Home will call. We'll come back to a fireplace . . . about here." He pulled her down on the bare concrete floor. "The children's rooms are down the hall. We'll have the intercom on in case they need us. But for now, this night, it will be just the two of us." He rolled on his back, cushioning her body with his. He framed her face with his hands. "How many shall we have?"

"I don't even know if I'll make a good mother. Besides, I'm getting too old for children."

He smiled, loving her courage and her fears. She was all woman. Strong as she was, she needed him. "You will. I know it, but if you don't want the patter of little feet, then we won't have any."

"You'd do that?"

"I'd do anything I have to, to keep you."

No one had ever believed in her so completely. No one had ever trusted her with his life as James was doing. The tears started again. He brushed at them with his thumbs.

"We could try one."

He pulled her down until their lips brushed. "Or two," he whispered before he kissed her.

Love. The greatest danger of all. The rewards were earned in tears and giving. Strength yielded to softness. Pride to caring. Two made one, stronger, better, richer for having taken that blind leap into the unknown future.

"Happy, darling?" James wrapped his arms around his wife, his hands spreading over the slight rounded mound of her stomach. Their child. Even now, the knowledge that it lay growing stronger every day inside her blooming body sent a shaft of wonder and thankfulness through him. One year. A lifetime and an instant. She had been his for one full year tonight.

Suzanne turned in the circle of his embrace. "We managed very well for strangers, didn't we?" she teased, her eyes dancing with wicked laughter. "We built a house, planned a huge wedding and made a baby without murdering each other."

He grinned down at her. "I distinctly remember you promising to do unspeakable things to my anatomy if I insisted on that green paint for the living room," he murmured, recalling one of their more colorful confrontations.

"It was a hideous shade of green, even the painter said so."

"I liked it."

"And you got your color."

He sighed, trying to look woebegone. "And I also had it repainted the next day. You were right. It was a hideous shade." He bent and lifted her in his arms. "And you've never let me forget it, either."

"A woman has to have certain little tricks to keep her man in line." The soft mattress cradled her body as he lowered her gently to the bed. She smiled at him, desire rippling through her with quiet strength. There wasn't a day that went by that she didn't know her luck in finding and having James in her life.

"You don't need any tricks, woman. I do. You run me ragged. It's a good thing I have a business that gives me a bit of freedom. Hong Kong last week. China next month. With your timing, we may end up with junior being born in a cab in Trafalgar Square."

Her fingers traced his smile. "Do you wish I—"

He stopped her with a kiss. "I don't want you any different than you are. I love you and the life we have created. You have the shop. We travel. Something I have always wanted to do and never taken the time. Until you, my life was wrapped up in the marketplace. Now I know about all kinds of people and cultures. I can't say I'm all that fond of some of the weird things you like to eat, and I'm definitely not fond of some of the plumbing facilities we've run into, but it has been interesting."

"How do you always know when I'm feeling insecure?"

"Practice and loving. You get that I-wish-I-were-average look in your eyes." He stroked the fiery hair back from her brow. "Every time you do, I want to tell you how much I love your uniqueness, how proud I am of your strengths and your abilities. Your I-dare-anything attitude doesn't worry me, though it does you. I like it. I like watching your eyes spark when you find something new or different. I like your mind when I tell you about my work and you ask questions and poke into issues, raising more questions."

"And I like knowing you're there to pick me up when I fall, to hold me when I scare myself to death reading some gory murder mystery."

He laughed at the last, hugging her tight while still being careful of their child. "I can't believe it even now. My wife, the woman who would wade into anything without thinking, can give herself nightmares reading about violence."

"It's not nice to make fun of my little idiosyncrasies," she reproved him, stifling her own grin. Her behavior was odd, to say the least. "I keep telling myself I'll give that kind of reading up, but then I see a new book out and down goes my resolution. Why don't you stop me next time? It must get tiring having me wake you up in the middle of the night."

James stared at her as if she had lost her mind. "Are you forgetting how we keep your nightmares at bay, darling?" he drawled.

Suzanne hadn't realized she could still blush. The heat ran under her skin, tinting it a soft pink as she read the memories of their passion in his hot gaze. "I remember," she breathed huskily, arching gently beneath him.

"The last thing I'm going to do is stop your habits." He pushed his hips against hers. "I like the results too much."

"So do I, lover. So do I."

* * * * *

Look for Ben's story, EYE OF THE STORM,
Desire #500, coming in June, 1989.

Keepsake